T0162560

THE SECRET OF
Caroline Rose

VICTORIA TURNER

authorHOUSE®

AuthorHouse™ UK Ltd.
500 Avebury Boulevard
Central Milton Keynes, MK9 2BE
www.authorhouse.co.uk
Phone: 08001974150

©2010 Victoria Turner. All rights reserved.

No part of this book may be reproduced, stored in a retrieval system, or transmitted by any means without the written permission of the author.

First published by AuthorHouse 7/29/2010

ISBN: 978-1-4520-4858-1 (sc)

This book is printed on acid-free paper.

This Story
is dedicated to the memory
of
'SISI'
(Empress Elisabeth of Austria)
(1837-1898)

whose portrait inspired the
character of

'CAROLINE ROSE'
also my late dear
mother and aunt
who always
encouraged
me to
write!

Where there is eternal light,
In the world where the sun is placed,
In that immortal, imperishable world,
Place me, O Soma!

Where King Vaivasvata reigns,
Where the secret place of heaven is,
Where the mighty waters are,
There make me immortal!

Where life is free, in the third heaven of heavens,
Where the worlds are radiant,
There make me immortal!

Where wishes and desires are,
Where the place of bright sun is,
Where there is freedom and delight,
There make me immortal!

Where there is happiness and delight,
Where joy and pleasure reside,
Where the desires of our desires are attained,
There make me Immortal!

Ancient Aryan Prayer

Chapter 1

At last the coach stopped in front of the Empress Hotel. Fuchsia Warwick thankfully rose from her seat, her body stiff after the long coach ride from the airport. She almost fell down the steps of the coach into the glare of the Karolian sunshine.

On her right gleamed the deep blue waves of Lake Raza, encircled by high mountains. So blue was the lake that it almost seemed as if the sky was below as well as above. On some days, Fuchsia was to discover, the lake was like a grey-black cauldron, the smoky mist rising from it like steam to curl and twist itself around the peaks in jagged wisps until it became one with the low-lying black clouds. But today, the first day of her holiday in Karolia – was golden.

She followed the other guests up a flight of stone steps through the terraced gardens to the hotel entrance. To Fuchsia's delight she was shown to a bedroom which overlooked the gardens and the lake beyond.

Later she stood before the mirror and stared critically at the pink skirt with a pattern of mauve flowers she had decided to wear that evening. She liked what she saw and finished off by applying pink/mauve lipstick and a touch of mauve eye shadow which gave violet depths to her vivid blue eyes. Then she brushed her waist-length fair hair until it shone and secured it with a pink bandeau. She was ready to go down to dinner. At 23 Fuchsia was already a successful artist. With the proceeds of her recent exhibition she had decided on a holiday in Karolia - a small European Kingdom she had always longed to visit after grandmother had told her so much about it. Late that night Fuchsia opened the windows onto the balcony and stepped out. She rested her arms on the rail, in a dreaming mood. Everything lay still and silent… The bright moonlight turned the lake and its encircling mountains into a huge silver mirror in a heavily carved silver frame and gave the trees and shrubs in the garden a white, ghostly radiance. All at once Fuchsia heard soft slow footsteps on the terrace below... She looked down and was suddenly very still, but curiously not in terror but more in wonder. On the terrace stood a young woman gazing across the lake and up to the mountains.

She wore a crinoline, layered in silk and gauze. The dress was encrusted in tiny diamond stars, and there were more diamond stars entwined in her long, glossy ringlets, and they glittered and sparkled silver fire, like some new starry galaxy in the moonlight.

The woman wore a stole loosely around her shoulders, and she clasped a fan. The woman slowly turned and looked over one shoulder. It was a beautiful face, but there was great sadness in the deep blue eyes. And then she was gone and only the lake shimmered in the moonlight.

Fuchsia was unable to move for several moments. Was it a ghost she had seen? She gave herself a hard mental shake - probably the woman was a guest in the hotel returning from a fancy dress ball. Yet Fuchsia thought, as long as she lived, she would never forget the bitter-sweetness that haunted that shimmering figure like distant music! The next morning she awoke heavy eyed... but soon cheered at the scene that met her eyes at the window. The lake and the sky were a perfect match in color, and Fuchsia's heart leapt in excitement as further along the lakeside she glimpsed the reddish brown towers and turrets of the mediaeval royal castle, the official residence of His Majesty King Alexander I of Karolia, last of the House of Raza.

Fuchsia remembered that a tour had been arranged for that morning to visit the royal castle, as some of the state rooms were open to the public on certain days. Although she was on holiday, Fuchsia noted with relish what an ideal subject the castle was for painting. She dressed quickly in a long cotton dress with a matching kerchief, the same blue as her eyes, and went down to breakfast.

"Will you please wait here everyone," called Lucian, the young fair-haired courier, who was in charge of Fuchsia's party. They were standing at the entrance to the covered wooden bridge that linked the rocky islet on which the castle stood with the mainland.

The fantastically uniformed guard stood to attention and allowed the party to pass along the bridge. Lucien caught up with Fuchsia who walked at the front of the group as they crossed the courtyard. The young courier had been pursuing Fuchsia since the journey started from the ferry, and although he was very attractive with grey eyes and an easy smile, his quarry was not particularly interested. He gave her a mock bow: "let me show you around my palace," he pleaded. Fuchsia laughed, completely unaware of how pretty she was when she did so.

"No thank you, I'll stick with the others." He withdrew, pretending to be offended, and began telling his charges the history of the castle. Fuchsia listened with interest, and walked admiringly around the seven-hundred year old building. Anything historic had always thrilled her. It had been built as a fortress stronghold and not even the rich tapestries and treasures or even the more modern apartments of the castle could conceal its basically grim aspect. On an upper floor, Fuchsia paused to look at an ornate vase, and so lost was she in her study of the object, she became separated from the others.

"Oh no," she gasped. She was in a bare stone corridor, but there were several doors through which they could have gone. She tried one or two, which proved to be locked. However, on trying the handle of the third one along, it opened and she found herself a thickly carpeted room lined with pictures.

She was just about to close the door again, when she caught sight of something so astonishing that she almost stumbled... Over the marble fireplace hung a full-length portrait of a beautiful woman, dressed in crinoline, diamond stars in her hair, looking over one shoulder with sad blue eyes... It was the same woman Fuchsia had seen on the hotel terrace the night before! So astonished was she that she did not hear the door close softly, or hear a smothered gasp, the next moment she was spun round, and hard demanding lips descended on her mouth and silenced her intended scream. For a moment she responded... a living flame seemed to ignite in her and erupt into a thousand colored lights. She had been kissed before... but never like this. Then she started to struggle and suddenly she was free. She stared at the man who had dared kiss her in such a fashion. He was very tall with black wavy hair, Slavic type features, and dark flashing eyes with lashes as long and thick as a girl's. He leaned against a chair, a red shirt open to his waist, exposing a tanned muscular chest, black hip-hugging trousers and a heavy gold ring on one well-shaped hand. He smiled showing magnificent white teeth. All at once the shock and surprise boiled up in Fuchsia, and with all her strength she brought back her hand and dealt the man a heavy blow across his cheek, and big as he was, it knocked him back into the chair. For a moment a terrible anger came into his eyes, and as quickly it disappeared, and he threw back his head and laughed. Then incredibly he took her hand and kissed it... "your pardon Mademoiselle... I thoroughly deserved your punishment."

He spoke perfect English with a slight accent. "I accept your apology," murmured Fuchsia, "but I think I ought to find my party now," and she turned to leave; "not so fast," drawled the man, "don't you want to know why I kissed your?" "Not particularly," answered Fuchsia with weary sarcasm. During her encounter she had forgotten the reason which had drawn her back into the room in the first place.

"Then why were you staring at that portrait?" the man asked her. Fuchsia faltered, "because, because I saw her on the hotel terrace last night!'" A strange look came into her companion's eyes, then as suddenly flickered and died, and he roared with laughter. "What is so funny," demanded Fuchsia.

"Look for yourself," he laughed, jabbing a long finger at the inscription of the picture frame. Fuchsia walked across and read slowly… "Caroline Rose 1840-1860, Queen of Karolia 1855 - 1860."

It was impossible! Yet the woman she had seen on the terrace had looked exactly like the one in the picture even down to the clothes and jewels! There could only be one answer… perhaps she was some kind of pathetic ghost… although Fuchsia knew she would most likely be ridiculed for voicing such a thought aloud.

"I suppose I was mistaken," murmured Fuchsia, "probably the woman had been to a fancy dress ball."

"This is why I kissed you!" He roughly thrust her in front of a mirror which hung on the opposite wall, his dark reflection swimming with her fair one in a silver-gold dazzle. His fingers bit cruelly into her shoulders. "Since I was a child I think," he began, "I have always been a little in love with Queen Caroline Rose… so… as a man… when I saw her double gazing at her portrait, my natural impulse was to kiss her very thoroughly!"

Her double! Fuchsia stared at her own reflection and then at the portrait. Yes it was true… except for a difference in coloring… the face of Caroline Rose could have been her own! "I must see you again…" the man behind her whispered passionately. Fuchsia backed away nervously. She answered… "I don't think it's very likely that you'll see me again," at once fascinated and irritated by his arrogant manner. He was unlike anyone she had ever met before.

He was, she admitted, the kind of man most women only dreamed about and were never lucky enough to meet in real life. She could almost hear her closest friend and flat mate Marianne telling her how mad she would be to give this marvelous looking man the 'cold shoulder'. Fuchsia was sorely tempted to agree to see him again.

"Have dinner with me tonight."

"You are very sure of yourself," Fuchsia remarked, a slight smile hovering about her lips.

"Will you have dinner with me if I tell you my name?" he grinned. Fuchsia nodded slowly.

"Call me Alex" the man said.

"Alex what?" asked Fuchsia.

"Just Alex for now," he finished. He showed her out into the main corridor and arranged to pick her up at the hotel at eight that evening.

Fuchsia ate her lunch at the hotel in a dream, her heart hammering painfully at the thought of several hours with the mysterious and devastating Alex. She spent the afternoon looking around the arcaded shops in the old town, the ancient stone houses dropping steeply down the mountainside, giving the illusion that they would topple 'higgledy piggledy' into the lake at any moment. Fuchsia came upon a little square, in the centre of which splashed a fountain surrounded by flower beds, delighting the senses with glorious color and heady fragrance. Tucked away in a corner of the square was a small boutique which caught Fuchsia's eye. In the window was displayed a filmy full-length evening dress of pearl grey with sleeves frilling about the wrists. Fuchsia knew the dress was made for her. It was exactly right for her dinner-date and possibly dancing later on. In the shop she went, and though the price produced a small gasp, she came out again the proud owner of the pearl grey dress.

Chapter 2

*S*he made her way across to a cafe and whiled away the time over delicious coffee, noting the many different nationalities of the passers-by. The sun was hot on her neck, but her eyes were shaded by a large blue straw hat which she had also purchased that afternoon.

She was pleased with the result of her careful preparations that evening. Her shining reflection gave back an attractive young woman, fair hair dressed high on her head, a touch of pearl eye shadow to complement her beautiful new dress which hissed like silken snakes as she turned this way and that. Lastly she picked up her silver evening bag, locked the door of her room and went down to the foyer which she reached on the stroke of eight from the old grandfather- clock which dominated the hall. Fuchsia encountered several admiring male glances.

The door of the foyer swung open and a big, dark, middle-aged man with a heavy moustache, dressed in a chauffeur's uniform strode through. He looked about him, inspecting the few women who sat in the lounge having an after-dinner drink, then his eyes rested on Fuchsia. He came over to where she waited. To her astonishment he clicked his heels and saluted.

"Mademoiselle Warwick?" he enquired, in a thick foreign accent. Fuchsia nodded. "Come with me please," and he turned on his heel back towards the exit.

"Hey… just a minute," began the girl, hurrying after him, "I am waiting here for…"

"Please Mademoiselle!" said the man impatiently and with a warning look in his eyes. "Your escort awaits you outside… please just follow me," and she was forced to run after him, trying to keep up with his long strides. A beautiful Rolls Royce was parked a little way up the road on the lake side, and Fuchsia realized with some nervousness that this was where the chauffeur was heading. Sure enough he opened the rear door with yet another salute, motioning Fuchsia to get in. Her heart gave a sharp thud as a deep masculine voice spoke from the interior of the car.

"So we meet again Miss Warwick!"

"Good evening," murmured Fuchsia, almost shyly. The mysterious Alex held out his hand to help her into the car. As he touched her arm, some sensation, far from unpleasant, seemed to shoot through her body, almost like an electric shock. She snatched her hand away, and for one ridiculous moment, from the way he was looking at her, she had the unnerving thought that he knew how his touch had affected her. She felt her face growing hot with, as she termed it, one of her 'idiotic' blushes. She was glad her face was in darkness.

She glanced at the man beside her. She could see his hard profile etched in the shadows like the statue of some pagan god in a dark grotto. He wore a dark dinner jacket, and a gleaming white shirt, which would, Fuchsia thought, do full justice to his copper- toned skin and outrageous good looks.

The car was travelling through the city streets by this time, at a steady pace. In the particularly narrow streets Fuchsia could see the cozy living rooms of the old houses, through windows with curtains not yet drawn, glass squares of warm golden glow, occasionally showing a family around the table eating their evening meal. Then they left the town behind, and across the lake could be seen the lights of another town resting on the side of the mountain, as if thousands of diamonds had been thrown carelessly on black velvet.

At last the car went through intricate wrought-iron gates into a long winding drive with tall trees that arched overhead like a leafy cathedral. A chalet-type villa came into view. The tires crunched on the gravel and came to a stop. For the first time since Fuchsia got into the car, Alex spoke.

"Welcome to my villa Fuchsia," he whispered and walked around the other side and held the door open for her to alight.

The heavily carved front door opened as if by magic, and an unsmiling manservant appeared from the depths of the hall. At the end of the hall, a staircase curved upwards out of sight, and Fuchsia's eyes were immediately drawn to a beautifully carved dragon rearing on hind legs, which formed the top of the newel post. The girl walked over and ran her hand appreciatively over the exquisite work of some long ago craftsman. "You like my family dragon?" queried Alex, raising an eyebrow. "Yes," answered Fuchsia, enthusiasm lighting up her face, "its lovely... as an artist of sorts myself I admire the work of other artists, especially such superior workmanship as this." A keen look came into the man's eyes. "Then you are a professional artist?" The girl turned to look at him. "Well yes...

I am, though not a very successful one as yet." Alex snapped his fingers. "Of course! I should have guessed, Fuchsia Warwick... I saw your exhibition in London recently. You underrate yourself. You are a fine painter. As a matter of fact I bought a small painting," he finished, pointing a finger.

Fuchsia looked and sure enough, on a wall opposite hung a small study in oils of the nephew and niece of her flat mate, painted in the garden of their home. It was one that Fuchsia had particularly enjoyed working on. All she could find to say however was... "I don't remember seeing you at the exhibition." "Well if had seen you, I would certainly have remembered," he said with a dark flame in the depths of his eyes. He threw open some double doors and Fuchsia strode after him, angry with herself for blushing every time he flirted with her, because that's all it was surely... flirting? She gave a small gasp as the room was revealed. The long windows stood open onto a small terrace. A little to the left of the window was a large grand piano with a piece of sheet music open as if someone had been playing. The view over the lake was breathtaking, large jeweled stars seemed to be drowning in the bottomless dark depths of the water and the total affect was of sky above and sky below.

"Beautiful," murmured Alex softly , handing her a glass of sherry.

"Thank you...yes very beautiful," she agreed, though she knew he had not been referring to the lake.

"Where do you live in England, Fuchsia?" he enquired.

"I share a flat in London," she answered.

"Where are your parents?"

"I don't remember my parents, they were teachers in Africa, and they both died of some local epidemic out there when I was a baby. I'd been left with my grandmother, my mother's mother that is… in England, and she brought me up and I lived with her until she died three years ago."

"You have no other relatives?"

"No, my mother was an only child and I believe my father was too, his parents died when he was very young. I'm afraid I'm all alone now."

"Have you a fiancé... a boyfriend perhaps?.." Alex persisted.

"No!" she said, "I only have my work plus a few close friends."

Alex said no more, just finished his drink, then the sour-faced manservant opened some doors which opened from the living room into the dining room and announced that dinner was about to be served. Fuchsia walked into the candlelit room where two places were set at the shining oval dining table. This room too had a beautiful view over Lake Raza. Fuchsia felt a little stab of unknown excitement as the candles threw blue black waving shadows onto Alexis curling dark hair. He gazed at Fuchsia from the other end of the table.

"My chef likes to experiment with dishes from many countries," he explained, "so I hope you do not favor just 'plain English food'."

"No," Fuchsia replied with a smile, "I like all kinds of foreign dishes, in fact I experiment quite a lot myself at home."

"Good!" he said with a short laugh. A maid entered with the first course, which was mushrooms 'Ile de France', a delicious mixture of mushrooms with eggs and cream, chilled, and spread on hot buttered toast. Alex smiled at Fuchsia's obvious enjoyment of the dish.

The main course was equally delicious being 'Angoumois Fish Stew' containing as the main ingredients, fish fillets, onions and dry white wine. Although the first two courses were French, the dessert proved to be a Hungarian concoction called 'Witches Froth', a dream of apples, egg-whites and brandy beaten together and served chilled. Accompanying the meal was a bottle of the excellent Raza wine. Finally to finish off with there was fragrant coffee.

After the meal was over, they rose from the table and nervously walked out onto the terrace where the girl kept her eyes fixed on the inky depths of the lake. She could feel him watching her in a way she both disliked and enjoyed all at once.

"Look at me Fuchsia," he whispered. She turned and trembled slightly as she encountered his devouring gaze.

"You enjoy my company... don't you," he went on. That was an understatement she thought with an inward laugh. Instead she said, "I've enjoyed this evening... so I suppose that must mean I've enjoyed your company." She knew what she had just said sounded a little ungracious, but her slightly off-hand manner was, she knew deep down, a defensive mechanism from the obvious attractions of this man. "You haven't said anything about yourself," the girl asked hesitantly after a while.

"It depends on what you would like to know," Alex answered still not shifting his disturbing gaze from her face.

"Well then… your surname for instance… your work... what were you doing in the palace this morning?" Fuchsia questioned boldly. A slight smile hovered about the man's lips.

"First of all my second name is… King... and to answer both of your other questions... I work in the palace in an official capacity."

"I see," said the girl, then a thought struck her. "Surely King is an English name?"

"Correct," Alex answered, "my father was an Englishman... he had made a fortune

from the business his father had started, and he was in Karolia on business when he met my mother at a ball given in his honor to which all the best families were invited. You see his business deal brought great prosperity to my country... for a while... not to mention the fortune he brought to my mother on her marriage. This villa was my father's home when he became a widower. My father has been dead these ten years... my mother... twenty year."

"And how old were you when your mother died?" questioned Fuchsia.

A gleam of amusement came into Alex's eyes.

"Ah I see, you are asking in your subtle feminine way how old I am. Well... I am thirty-five and I would have been fifteen when my mother died. These are my parents," he said indicating two silver-framed photographs on a table. Fuchsia walked over and picked up the one of his mother. Surprisingly she was fair-haired, but her eyes were those of Alex, and yet there was also a resemblance to someone else, only a very vague one, but the girl could not pinpoint it. His father had been handsome in a typically English kind of way, but his coloring was dark for an Englishman.

"Your mother was very beautiful," murmured Fuchsia. "What was her name?"

Alex replied, an expression in his eyes which perhaps reflected happier memories of his childhood. "She was called Zenobia... after the great warrior Queen of ancient times."

"A lovely face and a lovely name," added the girl. She replaced the photograph and idly picked out a couple of notes on the piano.

"Do you play?" asked Alex.

"A little," she answered cautiously. The man came and stood by the piano, looking down at her almost tenderly. "Please play for me," he said softly. Fuchsia seated herself on the stool, smoothing down her skirt, and trying desperately to avoid his passionate gaze.

"What would you like me to play?"

"Whatever you wish." So she began with the well-worn but beautiful piece 'Fur Elise' and drifted into a Chopin prelude and finally ended with a Strauss waltz. Something of the emotion she was feeling must have emerged as musical expression for she realized she had never played better. Although her playing was competent, she knew her limitations, her true and only vocation was the art of painting. There was a short silence when she took her hands from the keys, and then he said, "You play beautifully."

"Well I was well-trained perhaps," the girl assented, "but then my grandmother was a concert pianist and teacher, so I had a good instructor, I found my 'raison d'être' in another kind of art."

Chapter 3

She found herself suddenly silenced and her own eyes were held by his hypnotic gaze. The only sound was the slight swish of the lake against the rocks. For a fleeting second of time it seemed that all the dreams she had ever dreamed were encompassed in that gaze, dreams of art, love, ambition, hung motionless on the air creating for one second the perfect harmony that was fulfillment of self and the vision of total happiness. When the moment passed the girl knew without the slightest doubt in the depths of her being that she was deeply in love with this man, and it seemed to be a bitter sweet love, with an aura of intangible doom.

"Could your raison d'être be the art of love I wonder?" Alex murmured deliberately misinterpreting her last remark. "I will find out," he gasped, pulling Fuchsia against him.

"No... you mustn't," the girl protested, but he silenced her, placing a long finger against her lips, "you mean I must," he finished for her with the light of devilry in his eyes, and with a low moan she fell back against the piano, making the keys crash down in a discordant jangle. He crushed her against him and sought her lips hungrily, she responded as her senses were swirled into a whirlpool and a flaming mist of passion that raged like an inferno. When he at last drew away from her, she gazed back at him in a kind of golden daze. Then what he said shattered the tangible silence and her numbed senses into thousands of glass fragments.

"I love you Fuchsia. Will you marry me?"

The girl could only continue to stare. At last she found her voice.

"You must be crazy!" she blurted out, and to her horror she gave a shriek of laughter. The man seemed completely unmoved by her behavior.

"I may be crazy," he said with a smile, "but will you marry me?"

Fuchsia flopped onto the piano stool, gripping the edge of the piano with a grip of steel.

"I only met you this morning," she answered lamely.

"So?" whispered Alex with one eyebrow raised. "I repeat... my darling... will you marry me?"

And with the first snap decision of her life, Fuchsia answered "Yes".

The next day found Fuchsia by the lakeside soaking up the sunshine in a scarlet bikini which was greeted by many wolf-whistles as she took refuge from the heat under a huge striped umbrella. She still could not believe that the events of the previous evening had been real, that she had actually consented to marry someone she had known less than two days.

"I will be in touch," he had told her when he left her outside the hotel. In the meantime he warned her not to say anything to anyone about their association or future plans.

She held a sketch book on her knee, and idly she began to draw the arrogant dark features of the man she had agreed to marry. So engrossed was she in her task that she jumped when a pair of hands covered her eyes and whispered "Guess who?"

"Lucian! You idiot." She pulled his hands away in amused impatience. The young courier stared at the completed sketch over her shoulder.

"I see I have a rival!"

"What do you mean?" asked Fuchsia shakily, thinking for one ridiculous second that he had guessed her secret.

"Well isn't he then?" the young man laughed. "In that case prove it by coming with me to watch the procession tonight, and afterwards we'll dance the night away. What do you say?"

Fuchsia shook her head firmly. Lucien grinned though his eyes showed disappointment. "Oh well," he muttered, "I know Renata is only too willing to take your place," and he indicated an attractive brunette in a green swim-suit sitting on the edge of the swimming pool. She pretended to be busy swishing her feet through the water, but her face was marred by jealous fury as she watched Fuchsia and Lucien. Fuchsia looked away from the girl and back at Lucien.

"What is the procession in aid of?" she enquired casually. The man gave her an incredulous look.

"Why – it's probably the greatest event this summer, certainly it's a big tourist attraction. The procession is being held to celebrate the five-hundredth anniversary of the founding of the city by Jan Raza, first King of Karolia. Incidentally the King will be there tonight."

"What's he like?" asked the girl. Lucien pondered for a moment.

"Well - quite young, middle-thirties probably. He's very good looking; come to think of it he's not unlike your sketch. Though I wouldn't have thought there could be two such arrogant-looking devils!" he finished, laughing. A dawning suspicion began to whisper at the back of Fuchsia's mind, but she mentally squashed it quickly and finally for the suspicion was too fantastic to be even considered.

The atmosphere in the town and in the hotel that day was tense with excitement, there seemed to be hoards of extra people in the town by the late afternoon. It was very hot - too hot for comfort, and after lunch Fuchsia went up to her room, a severe headache pounding in her temples. She took a couple of aspirins and lay down in the dim coolness. She would rest this afternoon, for she did not intend to miss the night's festivities. She had forgotten her earlier fantastic suspicion and had at last agreed to watch the procession with Lucian, much to the girl Renata's fury. When the sun beamed its last rose-gold molten path across the lake, seeming to beckon dreamers to tiptoe along to the distant mountains, Fuchsia awoke, refreshed from her sleep, headache gone. She glanced at her wrist-watch lying on the bedside table. It showed five-o-clock; she leapt from the bed, she had one hour before Lucien came to collect her. Somehow she sensed she would not hear anything from Alex for several days, perhaps that was why she had agreed to go out with Lucien. She went into the bathroom and turned on the shower. She gasped as the red hot needles of water pricked her skin. She soaped herself thoroughly and washed her long hair in an herbal shampoo. Later, having dried her hair, she brushed it until was straight and shining, hanging around her like a golden cloak. The dress she selected from her wardrobe was a white, slightly Spanish-looking dress with scarlet flounces. She applied a touch of white eye shadow, and a scarlet lipstick which matched the red in her dress. Lastly, she took her hair back on one side and fastened it with a hair ornament, shaped like a large red flower. She was ready.

Silver stars had already begun to prick the dark blue sky, as Fuchsia, lifting the strap of her white bag onto her shoulder, crossed to the lakeside to wait for Lucien. But her thoughts were far from the attractive young courier, a darkly handsome face seemed to take form from the dark waves of the lake, and the gentle swish of the water seemed to sigh his name…

A lively marching song suddenly vibrated rhythmically through the stones of the old town, the notes marching bravely on into the dark waters of the lake which seemed to churn sluggishly in time with the music. Fuchsia raised her head to listen, and as the music changed to an old Italian air, her body and spirit soared to a pitch of electrifying excitement.

"Hi!" said a voice. Fuchsia turned to see Lucien smiling at her, looking very handsome in bright blue shirt.

"Hi!" she answered. He took her arm and they began to stroll along the lakeside towards the town where the procession would start. Already the main street was lined with crowds, children jumping up in the air to see over the heads of the adults. Lucien carved a path for Fuchsia and found a spot on the edge of the pavement. Already something was moving in a long line from the direction of the castle. At that moment a sleek red sports car came slowly round the bend in the road. As it passed Fuchsia, she saw it was driven by a beautiful haughty-looking girl with bright auburn hair coiled on top of her head. She was dressed in the blue and green national costume. Many of the people waved to her, but she ignored them, and accelerated out sight.

"Who was that?" Fuchsia shouted to Lucien above the noise.

"Lovely, isn't she?" Lucien shrugged. "If you like that haughty-looking type, she is, I suppose." Then he grinned. "But who she is is very interesting, for that is Elsa, Baroness von Kelberg, probably the future Austrian wife of the King!"

For some reason she could not think of, Fuchsia was depressed by that piece of information. Lucien carried on.

"Although the people may wave to her, she is not popular, she is known to be a snob, but the point is, as Queen Consort she would bring her money with her, and that is what the King and his country need. Unless of course he can get his hands on the fortune of the old Queen, Caroline Rose." Fuchsia jerked her head up in astonishment.

She quickly recovered herself, pretending to be only faintly interested. "Caroline Rose? What fortune?"

Lucien looked down at her, slightly surprised. "You want to hear the story?" Fuchsia shrugged. "Yes - why not, at least until the procession comes along."

Lucien pushed his hands deep into his pockets. "Well it all happened back around 1860, Karolia had a young and beautiful Queen, she inherited the throne from her father when she was only fifteen. The trouble was, she had been very delicate from birth, it was considered unlikely that she would ever marry and produce children, so it was taken for granted that her cousin Anna Maria would eventually succeed, which she in fact did. I don't know whether you know it Fuchsia, but the hotel your party is staying in was once Caroline Rose's villa. The castle was too damp for a person of her constitution. Anyway, for her eighteenth birthday, a portrait was commissioned, which now hangs in the castle but is not on display to the public (but I've seen it thought Fuchsia). The artist chosen was a handsome young Frenchman, Jean-Pierre Roland, little known today. Well - to cut a long story short, he and Caroline Rose fell in love, their love letters are still existence. But naturally, a marriage between a Queen and an artist was unthinkable. So Caroline Rose took the only alternative. She deserted her country and her people and eloped with the artist. Nothing was heard from her for two years, until at last agents of the new Queen, Anna Maria, found her dying in a Paris slum. Before she died, she told them that she and Jean Pierre had been married, that he was dead - and that she had given birth to a daughter! Her dying words were, 'you will find my child at...' and she died. They searched all over Europe, but not a trace of the child was ever found. If her parents had been married, she would not only have been the natural heir but the heir to the large fortune left to Caroline Rose by her English mother, and partly from the old King her father. Only the direct heirs of Caroline Rose could inherit the money, and then and only then, if her line died out, could Queen Anna Maria claim the fortune."

"Then," Fuchsia said, "King Alexander, as... presumably... the descendant of Anna Maria, could claim the money?"

"Correct!" nodded Lucien. "But first he would have to prove that there are no descendants of Caroline Rose livingly." Before Fuchsia could make any further comments, the excited shouts of children standing nearby heralded the approach of the first part of the procession, snaking along the road. First came the band, dressed in scarlet and gold, playing the stirring National Anthem. They were followed by the green uniformed Karolian Guard, mounted on black horses, tinkling bells on their bridles, the silvery sound harmonizing with the band. Then came the pageant of historical people and events in the country's past. A couple dressed in mediaeval clothes, representing Jan Raza, first King of Karolia, and his Consort, Queen Eva. Many floats went past carrying their 'monarchs' in a kaleidoscope of vibrant music and color, thrilling the artist in Fuchsia. The people cheered each passing scene, each one seeming to be better than the one before. Fuchsia and Lucien clapped and cheered along with their neighbors...

When the main part of the procession had gone by, there seemed to be an expectant hush, then a wave of cheering once more broke out from the people a good distance along the road.

"What's next?" whispered the girl to Lucien.

"Probably the royal party are approaching," answered Lucien.

Sure enough a handsome open carriage came into view, pulled by high- stepping, matching grey horses. Seated inside, quite alone, sat an elderly lady, white-haired, with aristocratic features, her dark eyes still beautiful. She inclined her head to the crowds as she went by.

"Who was that?" asked Fuchsia.

"That's Princess Irene, the Kings aunt," her companion replied.

Then suddenly the shouting rose to such a pitch that it almost deafened Fuchsia. She expected to see another member of the royal family come past judging by the amount of cheering - but it was not a member of the royal family, at least not a live one. Suddenly appearing as gorgeous as a costume-set from the heyday of Hollywood, came the most beautiful float Fuchsia had seen in her entire life. Like some exalted Jersey Battle of Flowers, the float was fashioned entirely of pink and white roses. In the centre of the float, beneath an arch of roses, was a vision that produced a small gasp of shock which Fuchsia quickly stifled. On the 'throne of roses' sat a girl dressed in an almost perfect replica of the diamond star gown of Queen Caroline Rose. The girl posing as Caroline Rose, though not the least bit like her except in general coloring, nevertheless with the clothes and makeup looked very like the tragic young Queen. The cheering, Fuchsia sensed, was not only for the splendor of the float but for the memory of girl of such radiant spirit that her personality lived on in the hearts of people whose great grandparents were only just born when that girl had been Queen.

Young girls followed the float dressed in beautiful pink rose-shaped tutus. They were students of the Raza School of Ballet, Fuchsia heard someone say in the crowd. They raised graceful arms like the petals of a rose blowing in the wind, their slender bodies swayed and pirouetted like the stem of a rose swaying in the summer breeze and lifting its beautiful face to the sun. The rest of the procession passed by then again arose ear-splitting cheering.

Along the road escorted by two more horsemen of the Karolian Guard, came a beautiful white stallion, carrying a black-haired man dressed in a beautiful uniform of midnight-blue. The horse's delicate hooves stepped proudly along, occasionally sidestepping.

"The King!" whispered Lucien. The horse reached the spot where Fuchsia and Lucien stood, so closely that its silky tail brushed Fuchsia's dress. The girl's head shot up to encounter the burning dark eyes of - not the King of Karolia - but the man she knew as Alex!

The horse and rider were long gone before the girl began to recover from the shock.

"What's the matter Fuchsia?" asked Lucien anxiously. "Are you ill?" The girl's face

19

was certainly chalk-white. The courier had noticed how the King had stared at the girl but then he had a reputation with girls, so that was nothing new.

"Did the King's looks completely overpower you?" he joked lightly.

Fuchsia smiled. "No I just felt a bit faint for second, that's all. I think the crowds and the heat…"

The young man began to steer her away from the onlookers.

"Yes - you're probably right. We'll go to a nice little open-air cafe that I know of, and you can have a long cool drink." The cafe, which overlooked the lake was nice and was encircled enchantingly by rose trees, the blossoms of which were a deep and glorious pink!

"How beautiful!" breathed Fuchsia. "I've never seen such beautiful roses."

"Well," said Lucien, drawing her down into a painted chair. "The clue in the name of the café." The girl glanced up at the sign over the cafe 'The Rose Queen' it read.

"What a pretty name."

"Yes," agreed Lucian, the cafe was called that because these roses, which grow all over Karolia were perfected in the same year as Caroline Rose succeeded to the throne, and so of course, the roses were called 'Caroline Rose'.

Chapter 4

The glorious perfume of the roses wafted across the girl in scented waves which she inhaled in ecstatic delight, as she sipped her lime-flavored long, cool drink which Lucien had ordered. The sound of music came from the lakeside and dancing couples whirled past them.

A girl came up to their table. She held a tray which contained velvet masks. She addressed Lucien: "You like to buy mask for you and lady - go dance – yes?" she said in very bad English, and pointed to the dancers who sure enough wore masks like the ones she was selling.

Lucien glanced at Fuchsia with laughter in his eyes. "You like mask? Go dance – yes?" Fuchsia nodded, trying to conceal her own laughter. He bought two masks - one for himself and one for Fuchsia. When the mask girl had gone, he gave Fuchsia a mock bow and whirled her across to the other couples in a lively Viennese waltz. It was a wonderful night and everyone was happy, even some of the more staid old folks were being pulled into the dance by mischievous young men and girls. Fuchsia found herself with many different partners, all strangers, though she could not be sure of that with their masks on, and in some cases, fancy dress.

The crowds seemed suddenly to grow thicker, her latest partner had just relinquished her, and the people jostled her, she became a little alarmed when she discovered Lucien was nowhere in sight.

"May I have this dance Mademoiselle?" She looked up into the dark eyes, gleaming behind his mask, a tall dark-haired man, wearing an open white shirt, with beautiful trousers of midnight blue. Straight away the sickening shock came back - the shock of realizing that the man with whom she had been foolish enough fall love with was none other than the King himself – Alex - Alexander, King of Karolia.

"Liar – cheat!" she screamed at him, "I never want to see you again." Blinded by tears she tried to tear herself away from his sudden embrace, but his arms might as well have been iron. To her horror, without saying one word, he swung her into arms and forced his way through the crowds, who stepped quickly aside at approach of the determined, powerfully-built man with a sobbing girl in his arms. He turned down a side street and there, waiting patiently, was the same beautiful white horse he had ridden in the procession. He swung himself into the saddle and lifted Fuchsia in front of him and none too gently. She clung to the horse's mane for dear life as he started off at a brisk trot in the direction of the lakeside, the water like liquid jet under the now dark sky. They soon left the streets of town behind, and horse was galloping along the lake road.

The animal's brilliant whiteness soaring against the black waters of the lake was like a brilliant shooting star soaring across the blackness of night.

"You can't carry me off like this." screamed Fuchsia into the wind.

"But I am carrying you off like this!" jeered her kidnapper, imitating her voice. Then he added in a low dangerous voice. "I shall do with you exactly as I please and what is more you will obey me! Especially since you now know who am!"

"I don't care if you're the Czar of Russia in disguise," snapped back the girl, recovering her spirit, "your 'sort' think they can do just as they like, well I'll have you know 'Your Majesty' that it may still be the Middle Ages here, but it's definitely the twentieth century in England!" She looked up at him and for one awful moment, with the soaring towers of the castle rearing up at them, his face bearing the dark demented beauty of a Count Dracula, for one awful moment she thought she was indeed in a medieval Transylvania and not modern Karolia!

At last the horse clattered over the covered bridge, Alex threw the reins to a man who came running from the shadows. Fuchsia shuddered in excitement, in spite of herself and the evening's revelations, as Alex deliberately lifted her into his arms and pressed her close, giving a low mockingly triumphant laugh, brushing his lips across her flaming cheeks.

He carried her into the castle, the girl struggling hopelessly against his superior strength. He kicked open a door and she saw it was the room where they had first met. He set her down in front of the portrait of Caroline Rose, which seemed to glow with an eerie radiance in the silvery moonlight which streamed through the window in rippling shadows, echoing the waters of the lake far below the walls. Then a flick of a light switch changed the silver to gold. He stood with his back to the door regarding her, his magnificent looks piercing her afresh like an electric shock. She shook herself mentally.

"What do you mean by bringing me here like this?" she stormed at him. He laughed, not a little put out by her anger.

"You know what I mean by bringing you here like this," he mimicked, "and what's more you thoroughly enjoyed being brought here like this - and like this," he added softly, pulling her down onto a couch and began to kiss her, such kisses as she had never known, and she responded to them until their mutual red-hot passion drugged her into a vibrant dreamland between sleeping and waking and ended in a violent crash of color as someone rapped sharply on the door.

Alex reluctantly raised his head and drew away from her. Fuchsia leaped up smoothing her hair, trying to smooth also her inner turmoil of emotions.

"Come in!" Alex called impatiently. A manservant entered, but betraying no surprise at the sight of the disheveled girl.

"Well, what is it," asked the King impatiently.

"Sir - the Baroness von Kelberg has just arrived, she's..." The same haughty auburn-haired girl who earlier had been driving the sports car pushed the servant aside and came through the doorway with a swish of blue and green skirts.

"Darling!" the girl cried, extending her blood-red tipped fingers to Alex. Her lover-like greeting died on her lips and she stopped dead in her tracks as her sharp black eyes pinpointed Fuchsia. The look on the face of the King could only be described as near maniacal fury! The Baroness pointed a finger at the English girl and said in German - in a harsh hissing voice, "Who is she?" When she saw the furious anger on the face of the King, she backed away a little. Fuchsia had retreated to the farthest corner of the room, if only the floor would swallow her up! But then she thought to herself - why should she let this woman humiliate her even if she was the King's fiancée. She stepped into the centre of the room and said in a firm voice – "My name is Fuchsia Warwick - Baroness von Kelberg!"

Alex took only what could be interpreted as a threatening step towards Elsa. "I think that answers your question Elsa - not that it's any of your business - NOW GET THE HELL OUT OF HERE – I'll tell you just once more as you seem to be both deaf and stupid - WE'RE FINISHED!" he yelled at her and pushed her roughly through the door.

"Alright, I'll go," she screamed at him, and then flashing a look of intense hatred at Fuchsia – "You'll pay for this, if it's the last thing I do!" and she swept from the room, her high-heels clicking menacingly down the corridor and into the distance.

Fuchsia sat down weakly in a chair, her anger at Alex forgotten by the shock of another woman's hatred.

"Why should she hate me so?" whispered the girl "why I don't even know her!" Alex stood in front of her and gazed down at Fuchsia with a strangely tender look in his jet black eyes. "She hates you - my darling - because you will be what she has hoped to be without any success - my wife... and my Queen."

The full realization of what he said suddenly hit Fuchsia - who he was - what he was. She jumped to her feet.

"This is ridiculous – I couldn't possibly marry you."

He caught hold of her arms "do - or do you not love me hmm?" he murmured in a husky voice.

Her face flamed at the look in his eyes. But she steeled herself to meet the look and answered without hesitation "yes – I do love you, that's the pity of it - but that's before I knew who you were."

"Should the fact of who I am change your feelings for me?"

"No of course not – I still love you as... as Alex but how could I possibly marry a King – it's not possible – me – a nobody! "Elsa is the kind a King should marry!"

He looked at her sternly. "Don't you think I should be the judge of that?"

She walked over to the window and stared at her dark reflection shadowed by a still darker, vibrant and exciting reflection which made her heart lurch not unpleasantly.

"Did Elsa know about me?" Fuchsia asked without turning round.

"She knew there was someone else - yes - but not your identity," Alex admitted. "I had already informed her that our engagement was at an end - but she wouldn't take no for an answer, but I believe the message has now been received loud and clear!"

Alex placed his hands on her shoulders, she shuddered at his touch. "Fuchsia," he whispered passionately, inches from her mouth, "Fuchsia - my love, marry me..."

"Yes!" she said for the second time as he devoured her with his kisses...

Hours later Fuchsia sat alone on the couch, gazing with brilliant glistening eyes into the painted eyes of Caroline Rose, whose eyes indeed seemed to hold a faint twinkle, almost as if the long dead Queen was amused by the passionate caresses of her royal successor and his future bride! Fuchsia rose to her feet and stood directly in front of the picture. "I wonder..." Fuchsia whispered with a soft laugh, "did you love Jean-Pierre as I love Alex?" Then a curious thing happened. The lights in the room seemed to grow dim, but the portrait seemed to glow with life and color and it was as if the figure moved and breathed and the long dead lips curved in a loving smile that seemed to whisper 'yes'.

The atmosphere became normal again, the lights were as bright as ever, but Fuchsia, whose face could have been that of the former Queen, but for her coloring, lay senseless on the floor, the strands of her long hair, spread out like golden threads against the rich red and blue pattern of the priceless carpet!

That was how the King found her when he returned some little time later from consulting with his private secretary about the details of the secret royal wedding which was to be solemnized the following day.

Chapter 5

$\mathcal{T}$he girl came to, choking as some fiery liquid was hurled down her throat like molten lava. Then her clouded senses cleared, and she realized Alex held a glass of brandy to her lips. She pushed it away and sat up. Alex helped her to her feet and she sank onto the couch.

"Fuchsia - what a shock you gave me." said Alex softly, "what happened?"

She remembered the cause of her fainting fit. "You'd never believe me," she answered shortly, "and you'd laugh!"

"Try me!" the King challenged.

Fuchsia stared at him for a second then said, "Suppose I told you that the portrait of Caroline Rose spoke!" Alex said nothing for a few moments, just considering the glass of brandy which he still held in his hand, but at least he did not laugh. Then he gave her an amazing answer... "you would not be the first one who had heard her speak…" Fuchsia's eyes grew wide in complete surprise.

"What did you say..." she stuttered. The King smiled wryly.

"Yes… my love… it is true, once many years ago when my mother was a young girl, so she told me, she was here in this very room, gazing at the picture as you were, no doubt, and suddenly she said the lips seemed to move and the whole figure come alive, and it seemed to say… 'Zenobia - you will be Queen' and sure enough the very next day, word was sent that the Crown Prince, my mother's eldest brother had been killed. That was during the First World War, and my mother did indeed succeed her father only a few years later."

"So it was also the ghost of Caroline Rose I saw at the hotel," whispered Fuchsia.

The King gave her a very curious look. "Possibly – I… have heard stories of her having been seen." Alex stared at the portrait for a long moment of time, almost as if he had forgotten the very existence of Fuchsia, who stood, waiting for him to speak.

At last, he straightened and said, almost abruptly - "Com!" He led the way along the corridor up a twisting staircase - up and up they went, with each step, penetrating deeper and deeper into the royal castle's past, until Fuchsia could almost smell those long gone times, could almost hear the pealing laughter of a long dead princess, almost hear the answering giggle of her long dead maid.

She nearly jumped out of her skin when Alex took her hand so lost was she in her reverie, and he pushed open a heavily carved door, and together they entered what had once been someone's bed-chamber. Fuchsia could almost feel the presence of the young girl who must once have slept here, for she was sure it had been a girl, Alex clicked on the light which immediately picked out the delicately embroidered hangings on the four-poster bed which stood at one end of the room. Whoever had once been the occupier of this room, had been definitely feminine. Fuchsia imagined how the exquisite pink and white carpet would look by the light of day, with the matching old but still beautiful wallpaper, the dressing table also of pink and white with its well used but still exquisite silver brushes and combs. A still silent Alex clicked off the light and went and opened long windows which opened onto a balcony. The fresh evening air immediately cut into the room's musty atmosphere like a shining knife into stale cheese. He drew Fuchsia onto the balcony to stand beside him. This room contained a view of the lake as yet new to Fuchsia. The lake had taken on the hue of grey-green, like a vast grassy expanse under the night sky. Across the other side of the lofty mountains had given way to gentle green hills but silhouetted even so by a dark mystery as old as time itself, while the moon sailed across a dusky sky, clouds, like wisps of smoke floated past its golden white face. Alex placed his hands on the girl's waist, until her heart seemed to choke at his nearness.

"She loved this view - so they say," the King murmured. "Can you guess whose room this was?" he asked the girl whose hair and face were silvered by the moonlight.

"Caroline Rose," Fuchsia answered softly.

"I will show you something." They went back indoors and he closed the windows and once more put on the lights. An ancient chest stood at the foot of the bed. Alex opened it, and after lifting layer after layer of soft material, he drew out something white and silky, but which time had made into something more the color of ivory. It was a Victorian crinoline, and in the folds of this silken Milky Way still shone dozens of tiny diamond stars. Alex held it up and the girl's heart gave a leap of excitement as she recognized the dress of her royal ghost and of the portrait. She took it from Alex and went over to a mirror and held against herself.

She turned to him her eyes rivaling the stars on the dress. "Could I..." she breathed.

He smiled at her pleasure, "Yes - try it on... but first..." he went over to the dressing table and opened a silver casket and drew out several hair ornaments, the diamond stars the dead Queen had worn in her hair. He slipped them from his palm onto the table-top.

"I'll wait outside," he said and closed the door behind him with a soft click.

Fuchsia hastily removed her own clothes and slipped on carefully and lovingly the beautiful dress. It might have been made for her. She twisted her hair into ringlets and entwined the diamonds in her shining curls. She knew what she would wear for a wedding dress. She put out the lights and went out onto the balcony and stood as another woman had done, looking out over the lake. Alex stepped onto the balcony, the black shadows sculpting his dark male beauty that would have inspired a Michelangelo.

The woman slowly turned and looked over one shoulder... it was a beautiful face... it might have been Caroline Rose... Alex stared at Fuchsia in amazement... she moved towards him... trembling...

"My darling," she whispered as he took her into his arms...

Centuries later, it seemed, Alex and Fuchsia walked back into the room and he closed the windows against the chill night air. With a start of surprise, she saw that all her luggage and belongings from the hotel stood near the door.

"But how?" she began.

The King raised an amused eyebrow. "I have very efficient servants," he murmured. A sudden thought struck Fuchsia. She shot Alex a suspicious look, almost one of alarm. She blushed as she realized he read her thoughts and was secretly amused by them.

"Do not stare at me in that old-fashioned way," he said, "for I assure you that my intentions are strictly honorable in an old-fashioned way. You will sleep in this room tonight alone, except perhaps for a ghost or two!" He quickly sobered as he saw her shiver. "Don't worry, I was only joking, that delightful but long dead Queen may still have her midnight fling, but - strangely enough - definitely not in the room she slept in. There will be however, a maid sleeping in the small room next door, should you want anything.

So don't think you are sleeping alone in the deserted wing of the castle." Without saying anything more he said goodnight and quietly closed the door, and Fuchsia stood all by herself on the pink and white carpet listening to the loud singing silence.

She awoke very early next morning, to see when stepping out on the balcony, the first beams of liquid gold sunshine stretching like glossy yellow ribbons across the surface of the blue-grey lake. The mountains were wrapped in a pearly candy-floss of white mist.

Fuchsia leaned on the balcony rail and looked over at the water lapping mysteriously at the ancient greenish grey stones at the base of the castle walls. A solitary rowing boat bobbed up and down a long way off, the person in the boat looking like a black dot or full stop. Within and without the castle was total silence, until a small brown sparrow alighted on the rail, and hopped towards Fuchsia, chirping excitedly, as if he knew it was her wedding day, and was offering congratulations. He looked at her hopefully from bright little eyes.

She went inside and emerged in a little while with the remains of a packet of chocolate biscuits which she found in her suitcase. "Here you are little friend," she called softly, and laid the crumbs along the rail, which very soon were snapped up by his beak, helped before very long by others of his feathered kind who landed beside him. Fuchsia watched the small birds in amusement until a loud knock on her bedroom door broke the restful atmosphere. She walked across the room and unlocked the door to find a maid standing there with a tray of early morning tea, a young woman with brown hair and soft brown eyes. It was the girl, who had slept in the next room the night before, and Alex had told Fuchsia that the maid's name was Greta, but that she could not speak English, but she did speak French. So Fuchsia who spoke quite good French greeted the girl in that language.

"Good morning Madame," the girl answered, "here is your tea - and..." she added, "may I offer congratulations?"

"Why thank you Greta!" returned Fuchsia with a warm smile. She was sipping her tea when the full impact of what her wedding would mean finally hit her. She almost dropped the cup as her tummy jumped in alarm. In a few hours she would be Queen of a country where she had expected to spend a few weeks holiday! A Queen! Her mind could not seem to grasp the idea, she must be dreaming! But she was not dreaming, she was here in the Royal Palace of Karolia and she would soon be the wife of its King. Another kind of excitement stabbed at her heart at the thought!

There was another knock at the door. "Come in," she called. Greta entered with something over her arm. It was an old but beautiful wedding veil, like the dress of Caroline Rose; it had become the color of old ivory. The delicate hand-made lace was of the stuff of dreams. "Oh it's lovely," Fuchsia breathed.

"His Majesty thought you might like to wear this with the dress," explained Greta, "he said it belonged to his great-grandmother, Queen Anna Maria, the cousin of Caroline Rose." Fuchsia smiled to herself, Alex could be thoughtful. She took the veil from the maid.

"Tell His Majesty that I shall certainly wear this gorgeous veil - and thank him," she added. The girl nodded and left the room.

She laid the veil on top of the dress where it was draped over a chair, a stray ray I sunshine lent it a pearly pink glow, until a cloud shadow once more reduced it to the color of old ivory.

Ten minutes later Fuchsia slipped down the corridor in search of a bathroom, she pushed open a couple of doors only to disclose more bedrooms, but at last, surprisingly in this ancient wing of the castle, she found a very modern bathroom. The walls were entirely of mirrors so that Fuchsia could see herself from all angles. A sunken bath of pink marble graced the pink tiled floor. The many pots and jars threw out a kaleidoscope of perfumes, which the girl breathed in ecstatically. Large fleecy pink towels hung from the heated towel rails, it was surely a bather's heaven! Fuchsia lowered herself into the bath, soaking and delighted by the soapy bubbly lather clinging to the water like little heaps of snow. Sometime later, emerging from the bath, she selected from a tall bottle a pink creamy shampoo, the color of which matched the soap and indeed the bathroom itself. She washed her long hair thoroughly in the pink basin and then toweled it until it was almost dry with a soft towel.

Back in her room, Fuchsia once more twisted her shining hair into ringlets, applied a pink lipstick and mascara then at last she once more slipped on the dress of Caroline Rose; she arranged the veil over her hair, and then in the full-length mirror to her amazement she saw a stranger… the pale lily bride of long tradition with dark pools of eyes stared back at her… the door opened softly, the maid stood there once more, but now dressed in blue lace, for she was to act as bridesmaid. She handed Fuchsia a large single cream rose, and a prayer book covered in cream velvet which she could carry.

"The ceremony Madam will be in the old Royal Chapel, in a short while, but in the meantime His Majesty asks that you wait in the Mermaid Garden where he will meet you shortly." She led Fuchsia down a flight of stairs and opened a side door which admitted the bright morning light. The girl blinked for a second adjusting her eyes to the stronger light - then she soon saw why the garden was so called. The garden, which lay to one side of the castle, overflowed with bushes of cream roses - such as the one she carried. Emerald green velvet of lawn surrounded the bushes and dropped in miniature terraces to the lakeside. But what caught the attention was a lily pond about half-way down the garden, which although not remarkable in itself, was the surrounding of one of the most exquisite statues Fuchsia had ever seen. On a natural rock in the middle of the pond sat a little mermaid gazing out towards the lake. Her profile disclosed the still childish beauty of a fifteen-year-old girl, her glorious curls springing to life from the stone itself, rioted around the upper half of her body and hung like a curtain down to her scaly fish's tail which snaked itself down the side of the rock. Her arms were outstretched in front of her, in one hand she held a mirror, and in the other a comb… yearning towards the shining water. Fuchsia could not tear her eyes away…

"So you have discovered our little mermaid," said a voice.

The girl turned and her heart leapt for Alex – the King - and her future husband stood not a foot away from her - resplendent in the gorgeous midnight-blue uniform he had worn in the parade, his black hair, curling over his brow. Fuchsia blushed, and he laughed in amusement… she tried to change the subject…

"Does this beautiful statue have a history?"

Alex gazed at it thoughtfully, "A certain Queen of Karolia loved the story of Hans Christian Andersen, which she discovered as a child. When she grew up and became Queen, she made a state visit to Copenhagen, saw their famous statue, and on returning home commissioned one of the world's greatest sculptors to create this statue - which he did although it no way resembles the one in Denmark." He stopped her as she was about to speak, "No it was not for once Caroline Rose, although it is said she once met the great Andersen, the Queen in this story was my mother, the late Queen Zenobia."

His eyes softened. "She loved this statue - and I think you will love it as she did," he added gazing at Fuchsia, and raising his hands he encircled her neck with a string of magnificent pearls.

He took her arm and led her into the ancient chapel, which lay curiously almost level with the lake. Its interior was largely Byzantine. In the long ago, the princes who had preceded the Kings of Karolia, produced a ruler who was the first to be converted to Christianity, and the teachings of Jesus reached Karolia much later than most other countries. The first Christian prince took as his bride a princess of holy Russia, who brought with her her own brand of Christianity.

An organ played softly as Fuchsia walked down the aisle, alone, except for her one bridesmaid. Her heart rose to a maddening crescendo as she saw her bridegroom looming nearer, whose face seemed almost impassive, until through the veil, she saw the dark flame in the depths of his eyes. His private secretary, acting as best man stood next to him. Fuchsia felt her arm firmly gripped and she realized she was at the altar, and the Bishop of Raza waited to marry her to a man she had only known a few days.

It all seemed dreamlike, as she repeated her vows in English, as indeed the service was in English for her benefit. It was all over very quickly and she was being led back into the castle on the arm of her husband.

They both sat down to a strange wedding breakfast - utterly without guests, only the secretary and the maid drank to their health and then speedily departed. The chef had surpassed himself with a three-tier wedding cake, but every inch of the white icing was shaped to form exquisite roses. They cut the cake together in the traditional way... but then sweetness of another kind was experienced... and the beautiful cake remained uneaten

Chapter 6

At mid-morning when the wedding breakfast had been cleared away, Alex suggested that they go rowing on the lake. Fuchsia stared at him in amazement, at the same time feeling something between relief and disappointment. He must have sensed something of what she was thinking, for though he spoke seriously, there was a suggestion of laughter in his eyes.

"I suppose you think it curious that I should wish to go rowing on my wedding day? Certainly it is unusual. But let me explain, although our feelings are strong, I believe it will be wiser, if for a time, we were not husband and wife, but an engaged couple, so that you will have a chance to adjust to your new position, for I am the first to admit that you have been rushed into a somewhat strange marriage, and it is not every day that a girl becomes a Queen. Also, you will come to know me better personally. Do you agree that this all makes sense?" Fuchsia nodded in agreement, although in one respect it seemed a little out of character with the type of man she thought her newly acquired husband to be!

But he was right, and she began to relax and feel some of the tension leave her, although she loved him she needed time to get to know him better, and she could still not take in the fact that she was a Queen! He carried on speaking... "for the next six months, no-one outside the palace circle will know that I am married, there will be no official or unofficial announcements, in fact to all intents and purposes, you are simply a guest in this castle. There are also other reasons for this which at the moment I cannot explain.

Fuchsia lay back in the boat and closed her eyes, the morning sun on her face. Alex rowed strongly across the water, plunging the oars into the purple-blue depths. In the distance could be seen a large steamer, crammed with tourists waving wildly, and pointing out places of interest. But their part of the lake was peaceful almost like the days when the world was young, when the gods walked the earth. Opening her eyes, the girl watched the man rowing, his lithe muscular body challenging the currents of the treacherous lake.

Was she a maiden carried off by Zeus? King of the Gods - how appropriate - Fuchsia laughed silently at her little joke. Who was Elsa? - Diana the huntress? Yes, Fuchsia could see her in that role very well. 'Now, now, don't be catty' she told herself in mock sternest. All at once she was aware that Alex had stopped rowing, and his face had paled beneath his tan.

"What's the matter – Alex?" she cried shrilly, alarmed by his manner.

"The boat's taking in water; it must have sprung a leak. It was very careless of the boatman not to have checked before we left." To her horror Fuchsia saw that there were already several inches of water in the bottom of the boat, and it was rising steadily.

"Baling out is no use, the water's coming in too fast."

"But why has it only just started to let in, why not when we first started off?"

"I believe we hit a rock back there," he said pointing back the way they had come, "It must have found a weak spot that wasn't actually a hole when we set off. It wasn't a hard knock, but it must just have been hard enough. Well - my darling, there's only one thing for it," judging the distance with his eyes, "it's not too far to the shore, we'll have to swim for it." The girl gave a low moan. "What's the matter, you'll only get a bit wet!"

"It's not getting wet I'm worried about," whispered Fuchsia, "but I'm afraid I can't swim!"

Before Alex could answer, they were both very suddenly washed overboard, not only by the rapidly rising water in their own boat, but by waves caused by the also sudden proximity of the pleasure steamer… all Fuchsia remembered was a rushing sound in her ears as she went under the treacherous water, she felt a strong arm grab her and then her head hit something hard and she knew no more…

"You'll be just fine honey, you just lie right there!" From a long way away, Fuchsia was dimly aware of a female voice with a decidedly American accent. She opened her eyes and found herself gazing up at an elderly typical American lady tourist, a straw sun hat perched incongruously on her elegantly-styled hair.

She and Alex, wherever he was, must have been rescued by the crew of the steamer, for she was lying on its deck. She sat up, someone had wrapped a blanket round her, a little group of people looked on with great interest. Where was Alex? She looked sideways. He was leaning against the rail, clothes drip - drip - dripping onto the wooden deck. He looked white and shaken, and for the first time since she had met him, she saw him smoking a cigarette. He looked somewhat relieved when she sat up and appeared to be apparently unhurt. She smiled at the American lady and thanked her for her consideration. She stood up and unsteadily took a few steps towards Alex who leapt forward to help her.

"What happened?" she asked. He drew on his cigarette, and then threw it over the side where bobbed away like a small toy boat.

"Well - to cut a long story short, we were tipped over the side of our boat, after your announcement that you couldn't swim and as I grabbed at you, you must have struck your head on the side of the boat, but luckily we were immediately picked up by the steamers crew who saw what happened!" The girl felt a sudden sharp pain across her eyes and everything went into a spin. She put a hand to her head. Alex put an arm around her.

"A doctor for you young woman," he said with an attempt at lightness. By this time the steamer was coming to the jetty, and people parted so they could be the first to disembark.

Back at the castle she was given a hot bath and then helped into bed. The doctor was sent for who said that apart from a nasty blow to her head there was nothing wrong that a few days in bed would not put right. Alex had left the room with the doctor, who gave the girl something to make her sleep. It had obviously worked, for when Fuchsia next awoke the room was filled with a blue-grey twilight, rippling water shadows on the walls from the uncurtained window, giving the impression of having been transported to a blue-green underwater world inhabited only by herself and the beautiful little mermaid, imprisoned in their coral palace with the wicked sea King.

Wicked - Fuchsia sat up with a start aroused I her own train of thought from her confused fantasies and the last wisps of the cotton wool clouds inside her head, making it ache abominably. Had Alex indeed married her for love? Or had he an ulterior motive that at the moment she could not even begin to guess at? Was the boat incident really the accident it appeared? Had someone deliberately created a weak spot in the boat knowing it would only take a couple of bumps to create a very considerable hole? But if so - then why? This Fuchsia could not answer, and gave herself a little shake, the atmosphere of the old palace was making her imagine things that were simply not there. She lay back against the pillows once more and closed her eyes until there was a knock at the door and Greta entered with some hot chicken soup which she encouraged

Fuchsia to eat and who surprisingly did not need much encouragement as she spooned it with great enjoyment.

She lay back on the pillows after Greta had cleared the things and carried the tray away, feeling another wave of drowsiness and a dull ache swim over her. Her head throbbed and she closed her eyes and slept.

Some hours later Fuchsia awoke once more, what had awakened her? Then she was aware that music was coming faintly to her ears from down the corridor. She peered closely at her wrist-watch, trying to focus her eyes. It showed three in the morning. Who could possibly be playing the harpsichord at that hour? She knew it was a harpsichord for she had seen it through an open door when she had gone in search of the bathroom. Greta said it was an old music room that had not been used in sixty years, although the instruments were attended to very frequently, by experts to keep them in perfect condition. Her mind gradually recognized the old English air 'Greensleeves' said by some to have been written by the Henry VIII for Anne Boleyn, mother of the great Elizabeth. It sounded strangely out of place in a mid-European castle, and played on a harpsichord. Her heart missed a beat and started to pound, she had to investigate. She slipped her feet over the side of the bed and pushed them into a pair of fluffy slippers, stood up and reached shakily for her dressing gown which lay across a bedside chair. Fuchsia tied the sash with a determined movement, and flicked on the light. She opened the door and blinked at the pitch darkness in the corridor.

Taking a deep breath, Fuchsia walked softly in the direction of the tinkling music which reverberated eerily around the cold stone walls, prickles of ice pin-pricked their way down the girl's spine as she got closer and closer to the source of the sound.

The door of the music room stood open, Fuchsia pushed it open further, and a shaft of pale moonlight burnished the polished wooden floor, spotlighting a figure seated at the old harpsichord, a figure with her back towards Fuchsia who stood rigid with terror, with that feeling of lead in her limbs, unable to move, as they spoke of in books. Fuchsia did not need to see the face of the player, for the apparition wore the dress she had only discarded that morning, for in the moonlight blinked diamond stars... and 'Greensleeves' had ended... the figure rose, turned, face veiled, and something else shone in the moonlight... gleamed wickedly with blue fire... it was a dagger flashing brighter and brighter as the veiled figure raised its eerie arm to strike a death blow at the living girl...

Fuchsia consumed with horror and unable to move as the knife stabbed downwards through the darkness of the room, down and down to her heart like a meteor to the earth... then a sound of light footsteps from behind... the swish of silk... an unknown hand dragged her backwards through the door, a knife clattered harmlessly to the floor... a muffled shriek left the unseen lips of the veiled figure who would have been her killer, and that killer seemed to melt into the wall, while Fuchsia once more felt her senses slipping away but before the welcome oblivion she felt fingers caress her cheek, like the touch of a gentle breeze on a summer's day.

The only person to witness that unseen helper was a large tabby and white cat that lurked in the shadows of the castle corridor, he watched the owner of the light footsteps pass by, with an understanding and knowledge gleaming in his large golden eyes, knowledge as old as the oldest pyramid and time itself.

Chapter 7

As the early morning light filtered through the window, Fuchsia's eyelids once more opened, at first her mind seemed a groggy blank, then flashed the memory of a knife slicing through the air, an unseen helper... and oblivion. She raised her head from the pillow, how had she got back to her bed? Her eyes slid across to the door, it stood wide open, a yawning oblong of blackness against the windowless corridor. Fuchsia's heart began to thud, a dark heavy shape with green lamps for eyes leered at her an inch from her nose, she opened her mouth to scream when the shape pressed its hairy body against her cheek, and a sound began deep within it until it became the roar of a motor bike... the scream became a wild uncontrollable giggle, the hideous hairy shape was the largest furry cat Fuchsia had ever encountered and the motor bike purr lulled her to sleep as it settled down beside her in the warmth of the bedclothes.

She awoke once more with sunlight streaming into the room and Greta shooing the cat off the bed.

"No... please leave him!" exclaimed Fuchsia, but the cat had already gone, through the door like lightening. The girl sat up in bed as the maid placed the breakfast tray across her knees.

"I didn't know there was a cat in the castle," she said with pleasure, for the other great love in her life apart from painting was cats. "What do you call him?" The maid shrugged reflecting the attitude of so many foreigners that animals were less than nothing.

"He is called Tiger, he belonged to the housekeeper, but she died, but the King is fond of cats so he allowed her pet to stay; he is only supposed to be in the kitchen, but he wanders about until he is shooed back."

Fuchsia wondered what the maid's reaction would be if she told her someone had tried to murder her during the night. She would not be believed.

"Where is the King?" she asked Greta as she got out of bed.

"Oh Your Majesty... I almost forgot... His Majesty gave me an important message for you, he said he was sincerely sorry but he was called away to Paris late last night on matters of state, and he will be away at least a month." Fuchsia looked at the girl, thunderstruck with amazement and a kind of cold fear.

"He's gone?" she said stupidly.

"Yes maam, it was so urgent he had to leave without even seeing you... but he said he will be in touch... very soon." The girl thanked her and went to the bathroom in a kind of frozen daze. What was so urgent that he left her only one day after their wedding? Was it genuine business... or did he find it impossible to control his feelings... for as she knew from her own point of view, his presence both terrified and thrilled her at the same time.

What was terrifying her at this moment was the fact that some-one wanted her head... but who and why? There was no-one she could turn to... Alex would have been the obvious choice... unless... though God forbid... unless he was the killer! But that figure at the harpsichord had definitely been a woman, if it was a man it was a very short man not Alex's six foot plus! And why would Alex want to kill her when he had just married her? Unless there was some as yet unknown reason. She shivered and stepped into the bath.

In the days that followed Fuchsia was very much alone, the only people she saw were her maid and the servants who waited at table. She had discovered that to one side of the Mermaid Garden was a swimming pool and in this she spent most of the hot empty days that lay ahead. She also made small sketches of the birds that wheeled high over the lake, and started a small oil painting from the drawing she had made of Alex. In the evening after dinner was over it became her habit to sit in a comfortable armchair in the extensive library where she discovered a rather ancient 'English/ Karolian – Karolian/English dictionary because obviously she had to start learning the language at some point, though at the moment mainly to converse with the servants. In a matter of days she picked up quite a few useful phrases and even began to catch a word here and there when the maids were talking among themselves.

There were color television sets in many of the private apartments, but apart from the occasional film in English, French or Italian which latter language she also spoke a little, there was not much point in watching television until she had at least a working knowledge of the language.

The nights she came to dread. She had taken to locking her door and even dragging over a heavy antique wooden chair from a small adjoining room which had once been the powder closet of an eighteenth-century Queen. She did have one companion to share the long nights. Tiger the tabby cat who seemed to have taken a fancy to Fuchsia, and indeed the feeling was mutual. He seemed to know when she was preparing for bed and there he would be all curled up on one side of the bed, and there he stayed until the door was unlocked the following morning. Sometimes he joined her in the library when he would leap onto her lap and decide that her book was the thing to sit on.

As the days went by, Fuchsia became more and more relaxed; after all it was possible that the crack on the head she had received during the boat incident had caused her to imagine the events of the following night. One day, with Tiger at her heels she went into the old music room and gingerly struck a key, it was in perfect tune, she sat down and began to play the tune she had heard on it, 'Greensleeves'. Tiger thoroughly approved, for he rolled on his back, his mouth opening in short squeaky mews and purring ecstatically.

The girl soon forgot her surroundings, liking the tinkling sound of the harpsichord. Her grandmother had once possessed such an instrument, not such a fine one of course, but beautiful nonetheless. She had learned to play both piano and harpsichord, the outcome of which was a quite formidable technique, although she did not have a gift for it as did her grandmother. Suddenly as she was playing the years seemed to roll back and her Grandma was playing the same melody on her harpsichord, and she was telling the child about a beautiful rose, a very rare rose... then the memory vanished as quickly as had come. She shook her head, trying to recall it, but to no purpose. She shrugged and carried on playing, right through the repertoire of pieces she knew by heart.

She did not notice the shadows lengthening outside, the little mermaid becoming a dark aquatic shape against the horizon, for the music room overlooked the Mermaid Garden; she did not see anything until Tiger hissed at something through the dark window, his fur bristling, his tail like a fox's brush. Fuchsia's inside somersaulted, her hands dropped shakily from the keys. She walked across to the window and saw with paralyzing fascination what the cat saw... for as they both watched, the dark shape of the little mermaid stood upright and then slithered like a huge fish to the edge of the lake, and dived in with a distant splash!

She stared, her eyes locked on the empty rock where the mermaid had rested. Was she mad? If that was so, the cat was mad too! Someone in this castle was playing a strange kind of game, with what motive or purpose she knew not. First the boat, then the veiled figure, and what of the third party who saved her, a party of whom the harpsichord player had appeared to be terrified. Now a statue had apparently come to life. Once or perhaps twice someone had tried to kill her or with the latest incident to gradually drive her insane. Who and why? What had begun as a dream holiday with a fairy tale ending was changing to a nightmare. Apart from locking herself in her room night and day there was nothing she could do about it at least until Alex returned, and even he might well be involved. Whoever the 'someone' was they knew every move she made, the person had known she would be in the music room, so there must be somebody constantly watching her. Fuchsia shivered, she did not like the idea of a pair of eyes, eyes she herself could not see, following her everywhere she went.

She had to protect herself, until such time as she found someone to trust, who that person would be she did not know.

The answer to her silent question was to come sooner than expected. She went back to her room and switched on the light, sat down at the dressing table and began to brush her long hair, glistening like gold copper under the glow of the table lamp. There was a knock at the door, Tiger sprawled lazily on the bed but opened one eye to see who might dare to knock the door.

"Come in," Fuchsia called. A maid entered and bobbed a curtsy.

"There is a telephone call for you maam, in the library." The girl looked astonished... "A telephone call for me?"

"Yes maam, a young man, an Englishman." Fuchsia's heart leapt.

"An Englishman?" the girl echoed. Then it could only be one person thought Fuchsia as she hurried along with the maid to the library. Lucian, the courier from the hotel! The one person she could trust. She picked up the receiver.

"Hello." To her surprise a rather cold voice came onto the line and answered her.

"Miss Fuchsia Warwick I presume?"

"Yes. Is that Lucien?" she said.

"Yes it is, and I think you have a lot of explaining to do!" The girl started to feel angry at the tone of his voice.

"Just what do you mean by that?"

"I think you probably know the answer to that. But for a start, what do you mean by just walking out of the hotel without a word to anyone, all I knew about it was when that fierce looking chauffeur asked the chambermaid to pack your clothes, and then he made off with your suitcases minus an explanation. I had to step right into his path to get any kind of information. All he said was that you were staying at the castle. Of course, after I had given it some thought I remembered the way the King had stared at you at the procession, your reaction and that clever little sketch you had drawn, so naturally I put two and two together..."

"And came up with the wrong answer!" she finished for him angrily.

"Was it?" Lucien drawled slightly sarcastic.

"Yes it was. I think you might have given me the benefit of the doubt!"

"Alright, I will, why are you staying at the castle, if it isn't at and for the pleasure of his high and mightiness, his royal arrogance, King Alex?"

"I can't explain why I'm staying in the castle, at least not on the telephone. Perhaps I could meet you?"

"OK," Lucien answered in a bored drawl. "When and where?"

Fuchsia gripped the receiver and thought hard. Where could they meet without being seen? Of course - the side gate into the Mermaid Garden! It was never locked. She explained to the courier how to find the gate. He arranged to meet her there at eleven o'clock that night. She replaced the receiver, her heart pounding. After dinner she changed her dress for a pair of dark grey slacks and dark colored jersey, so anyone who happened to be watching would find it extra difficult to locate her in the dark.

Eleven o'clock came; the chimes rang out from the various clocks in the state apartments. She walked across the garden, the old gate creaked open, Lucien stood there in the shadows. He quietly closed the gate behind him. They looked at each other unsmiling.

"Hello Lucien," whispered Fuchsia. The man did not answer but just threw down his cigarette with a kind of childish fury and stubbed it out on the gravel path. The girl noted the action but decided to ignore it and checked her rising temper.

"Well!" he managed to get out at last. Fuchsia sank down onto a nearby stone seat. There is no point in telling you anything unless you at least meet me half way!" she answered. The man stared at the ground, "alright" he agreed. "Fire away."

"It all started the day of the tour around the castle," Fuchsia began. Lucien nodded.

"I guessed as much, especially after you got 'lost'."

"I just happened to meet him, purely by accident... and it..." she stuttered.

"Love at first sight!" jeered Lucien. Fuchsia colored hotly in spite of herself and was glad of the enveloping darkness... but the man suddenly grabbed at her and embraced her roughly, seeking her lips, inwardly and outwardly she shrank from his touch, twisting her head from side to side to avoid his unwelcome kisses. He was still stronger than her. She tried in vain to get away from his now nauseating touch but he only held her closer, and she began to get very frightened! He must have gone crazy with jealousy.

If she screamed she would bring the servants running and that was something she did not want except as a last resort. So she did the only other thing she could think of... she stamped hard on his foot with her high-heeled shoe which she had forgotten to change out of, and for good measure she kicked him in the shins! He at once let her go with a gasp of pain and crumpled up onto the seat which she had just vacated.

"How dare you!" she breathed in a low but furious tone. "If this is the way the King carries on and as you seem to know all about it - well they say it takes one to know one!" She was jeering at him but she did not like to think what might have happened had she been unable to stop him. In the ordinary way he was probably quite a nice decent young man, but that jealous rage mixed with something else was too much.

As Fuchsia watched him, he seemed to calm down, and eventually he was still and silent. The silence seemed to grow longer and longer, but at length he stood up and faced her.

"Please forgive me; I don't know what came over me." He put out a hand and the girl took a wary step backwards.

"No - please - it won't happen again," he gasped.

"It had better not," Fuchsia answered, tight lipped. Then it was her turn once more to sit down on the stone seat.

"I need your help," she said. Then she told him everything from the meeting in the room of the portrait to the present moment, the attempts on her life and the 'ghostly' experiences. He was very subdued when she had finished, and very astonished.

"You mean you've actually married him?" he gasped out.

"Yes - of course," she answered. "I suppose you don't believe the supernatural part," Lucien looked down at his feet, considering.

"Well - it is rather hard to swallow, but on the other hand there seems to be quite a lot of belief in that kind of thing nowadays, and to be honest I have heard of such a story in connection with the Empress Hotel. But I do have the feeling that the ghost playing the harpsichord was very much human! And as for the walking statue - let's just try a little experiment! He gave her a little grin, a rather sheepish grin in fact. He set off towards the Little Mermaid on her rock. The man took hold of the statue round the waist where her fish tail began and after much heaving he moved the statue to one side of the rock, and then with another great effort moved it back again.

"You see?" he grinned. "It was just as I thought, with perhaps two or three people it would be possible to remove this statue from the rock, and no doubt from the windows in the castle, especially when it is getting dark, a woman or even a man in the appropriate costume, could take the part of a very convincing 'mermaid' come to life, scaring the wits out of anyone who might be watching, especially one as sensitive to atmosphere as you are!"

Fuchsia gave a nervous little laugh! "Well, at least I'm relieved I'm not seeing things or going mad," she said in a low tone.

"You are most certainly not going mad," Lucien echoed. "But I do think someone is mad enough to want you out of the way."

"But who could it possibly be? And why?" They stared at one another. Lucien dropped his eyes.

"I hate to say this, and I hasten to add, I must say it, but completely without prejudice on my part, there is one person who might want you out of the way - and that person is the King." The girl's eyes flew wide. She was visibly shaken.

"But why?"

"I think I might have a slight clue to the 'why', and it could be the motive of other possible suspects as well as the King. I have a notion that there are probably two or even three people involved in any case."

"What is the clue?"

"I think the clue is in the old story about the fortune of Caroline Rose!" The girl was completely mystified.

"How could that possibly concern me?" Lucien did not answer immediately. He just looked rather serious and slightly puzzled.

"Tell me," he began, "what do you know about your immediate ancestors?" Fuchsia looked startled:

"Well - which side?"

"Any side?" Fuchsia took a deep breath.

"My father I know absolutely nothing about. He and my mother were both students when they met, his parents died when he was very young and I suspect he was raised in a foster home. I don't even remember him, he and my mother died when I was a baby. The only person I knew well was my grandmother, and farther back than that I know very little. My grandmother never spoke of me having any distant relatives like cousins and so on, so I just assumed I had none. I don't even know who my grandfather was, not even his name."

"Didn't it ever strike you as a bit odd, not knowing anything?"

"I just didn't think about it. I had my grandmother and that was it.

"What was your mother's maiden name? And do you know what your grandmother's maiden name was?"

"My mother's maiden name was Peters, which of course was also my grandmother's name. If she had a maiden name I don't know what it was. I begin to wonder if perhaps my grandmother had my own mother outside marriage. It is more than possible." She paused and then went on:

"Grandma was a concert pianist and it is very likely that she met someone who was perhaps socially superior whom she could not marry, and who was in fact my grandfather." Suddenly the vague memory Fuchsia had had while at the harpsichord came back to her in more detail, her grandmother's voice echoed down the years... "We were all named for flowers, she so loved flowers, and a wonderful rose was named after her... I was called Primrose, you are Fuchsia, your mother was Lily and my own Mama was Gentian..." That was it! Her great grandmother's name was Gentian! She hurriedly told Lucien what she had remembered. There was a curious kind of excitement about him as she finished repeating her grandmothers words and left through the side door, promising to get in touch with her before long.

Chapter 8

When Fuchsia arrived back in her room, all kinds of wild possibilities chased themselves crazily round and round in her brain. What was the idea that Lucien had at the back of his mind? Did he somehow think she could be linked in some way with Caroline Rose? But how could that be? She suddenly had an idea. Perhaps it might help if she read a little on the background of Caroline Rose and past members of the Royal Family.

She made her way downstairs to the library, and cast her eye over the vast collection of books there. Before long she found what she was looking for, and in English too, 'A History of the House of Raza'. It was a heavy book, and she placed it on the long oak table, and eagerly turned to the section covering the nineteenth and early twentieth century. She found some quite interesting facts concerning the background of Queen Caroline Rose and various members of her family. Caroline Rose's mother, for instance, another Caroline had been English, a daughter of the first Duke of Berrington. It appeared that she had been his only child and she inherited his vast fortune on his death, although the title died out. Her Somerset home, Combe House, Fuchsia knew well, for it now belonged to the National Trust. This was most certainly the vast fortune that would have been inherited by Caroline Rose.

Another interesting fact turned up. Frederick III, the father of Caroline Rose, had, for some unknown reason, directed on his deathbed that should his daughter die without issue, his sister Anna Theresa should be excluded from the succession and that it should pass to her daughter, Anna Maria. The writer did not say why. Anna Theresa also had a younger daughter from a second marriage, Carlotta Elisabeth, whose own daughter became the second wife of Anna Maria's son, Jan VI, and the mother of Alex's aunt, Princess Irene.

What complicated relationships they had in royal families the girl thought. At the back of the book was a genealogical chart, or otherwise family tree of the House of Raza. By reading the text and constantly looking back at the chart, Fuchsia eventually acquired a mental picture of the various branches. She noted the position of Alex on his family tree and with some amusement saw that his father's surname really had been King. Some coincidence! His mother, Queen Zenobia had been at the advanced age of forty eight no less when her son was born, her first and only child after eighteen years of marriage. Alex - as he had said - was fifteen when she died.

One fact which seemed to leap at her from the text was that apparently in Karolia the eldest child of the sovereign succeeded regardless of whether they were male or female, although female successors seemed to be more popular. Perhaps because a Queen commands an aura of romance and fervor of patriotism which no King can ever match. After all thought Fuchsia, people only remember Henry VIII for his six wives, Charles I because he had his head chopped off, yet everyone remembers Elizabeth I and Victoria because they gave England two golden ages, the greatest ages and people that English men and women, and indeed the world had ever known. A King in petticoats had made Philip of Spain hide under his bed for fear; the daughter of Anne Boleyn had smashed his Armada with glee! Who needed Kings with Queens like that? Well perhaps one King - called Alex, thought the girl.

What puzzled Fuchsia was the silence on the part of the book about the reason for excluding Anna Theresa, the aunt of Caroline Rose from the succession. Had the King of that time known something about his sister that perhaps historians did not? Fuchsia looked back at the family tree. On closer inspection she saw that Anna Theresa had only been the half-sister of King Frederick, her mother being his father's second wife, Giulia Caravari of Genoa. There appeared to have been quite a few second marriages in the family and marriages between cousins. Fuchsia's head began to ache trying to sort it all out. She closed the book with a snap, and as she did so something slipped from between the pages and fluttered to the floor, a piece of paper, yellowed with age. The girl stared at it for a second or two and then bent down as picked it up. She turned it over; the paper was certainly old with some barely decipherable handwriting. The rather jagged piece of paper appeared to have been torn from a diary but the odd thing was that the tear looked quite recent, so obviously someone had the diary to which the paper belonged and for reasons of their own had ripped it out. Fuchsia peered closely at the writing. She instinctively felt that it was a young hand... a girl's hand... it read... 'I sense her hatred... and I am afraid...

I believe my father was right about her... why did I not listen to him... to his warnings that she...' and there it ended, at that important point an unknown someone had ripped it out.

Fuchsia suddenly felt that she had stumbled on something important. She examined the paper again. Although the page had been jaggedly torn from the unknown diary, the sheet had again been torn in two, at the point where the writer had concluded the sentence, in short, after the words that 'she...' The girl felt that the end of that sentence would explain a lot. Therefore somewhere, unless it had been destroyed, the bottom of the sheet of paper lay hidden or lost. Who had the writer been? Who was 'my father'? Who was she whom the writer feared so much? There were many questions that needed answering, many skeletons in the cupboard that needed to be identified before the mystery could be cleared up, before Fuchsia could breathe freely again without the threat of an unknown killer!

At last Fuchsia replaced the piece of paper inside the book as she had decided that the safest place for the paper would be where she had found it. But, however, she pushed the book to the back of the shelf where it was not so noticeable. She then had a sudden thought. Although she had seen the mysterious and beautiful portrait of Caroline Rose, she had not seen likenesses of the other characters in the drama, apart from the photographs of Alex's parents. She emerged from the library, walked down the corridor a short distance, opened a pair of double doors and stepped into the eerie silence of the portrait gallery. As many of the rooms in the palace did, it faced the lake, and the rippling light from the long windows lent a strange luminous animation to the painted likenesses of people of who only memories remained but whose blood continued and surged anew in the life force of Alex. As these thoughts passed through the mind of Fuchsia, she herself felt a sudden tug in the depths of her being, feeling in her blood and in her soul that eternal physical and mental link with her unknown ancestors who had walked this earth hundreds and thousands of years ago who were part of her and responsible for her very existence, all those people had given her life.

She felt for the switch, flooding the gallery with light, destroying all eerie illusions. She passed the early portraits, stiff men and women of the sixteenth century, with Elizabethan ruffs and farthingales, and went on to the seventeenth century, where one portrait caught her eye. It was, according to the plaque beneath, a certain Princess Charlotte, youngest daughter of Queen Eva II. This Queen Eva had once visited the Court of France, where beside Louis XIV; she had met a certain Charles Stuart future

Charles II of England. No wonder, thought Fuchsia, Eva's daughter bore more than a passing resemblance to the 'Merry Monarch'.

Eventually she came to the nineteenth century, and paused before the portrait of Frederick III. He had been a tall, fair-haired man, but with dark brown eyes. He looked shrewd yet kind. Next to him hung the portrait of his English wife, Caroline, and of these two, the parents of Caroline Rose, their daughter had favored her mother, the same bright chestnut hair, the deep blue eyes, the smiling mouth. There was a blank space next to these portraits, and Fuchsia guessed that the beautiful birthday portrait of Caroline Rose had once hung here.

Moving along she came to a painting of what at first glance appeared to be that of a black-haired woman with handsome features until Fuchsia looked at the eyes. They were dark, almost black, but they were the coldest eyes Fuchsia had ever seen, even the room seemed suddenly to go colder. They were hypnotic in their coldness, with a dark nameless quality in their depths. The girl almost dragged her eyes away to the plaque beneath. It read: 'Anna Theresa, sister of Frederick III, mother of Queen Anna Maria'. So this was the woman who had been deliberately excluded from the succession by her own brother! Fuchsia, although she could not yet say why, silently agreed with the long dead King's decision. A woman so utterly different from her brother - but then she was only his half-sister. A woman according to the library source whose Italian mother carried the blood of the Medici and the Borgia's in her veins! Powerful ingredients for evil - came the sudden thought into Fuchsia's mind. She gave herself a little shake and passed on to the next picture.

The next painting made Fuchsia gasp, for though the face in the picture was that of a woman, it was the face of Alex! The same black wavy hair, the Slavic features, the dark flashing eyes! The plaque told her that she was looking at Queen Anna Maria, the Queen who succeeded Caroline Rose, the great grandmother of Alex. There was no trace of the cold eyed woman who was her mother in the face of Anna Maria. The eyes were warm and full of life - but - it was the face of one who loved pleasure rather than duty, perhaps one who had not really desired the position in which she found herself, into which circumstances had forced her. Fuchsia discerned a lack of ambition in that warm but pleasure-loving countenance. Fuchsia spared no more than a glance for the portrait of her husband, a Karolian count, and scarcely more for the handsome but rather weak features of her son Jan VI. She looked briefly at Prince Alexander, Alex's uncle who had been killed in the Great War, and came at last to Queen Zenobia, who she suddenly realized with a start, had she lived, would have been her mother-in-law. Zenobia s eyes, as she had noted before, were like those of Alex, and now she had seen the portrait, like those of Anna Maria. But her hair was a golden color, and again Fuchsia was put in mind of someone else, someone she knew well. Suddenly an image flashed into her mind, a photograph she had seen long ago, of a laughing young woman holding a little girl. It was this young woman whom Zenobia reminded her of, and then it came to her, for that young woman was Fuchsia's grandmother, and the little girl was Fuchsia's own mother as a child! Zenobia was a younger version of the old lady who had raised Fuchsia!

What Lucien had hinted at then at last hit the girl in the deserted gallery, it could not be a coincidence that she herself resembled Caroline Rose, that her grandmother resembled Zenobia, somewhere ordinary Fuchsia shared a blood tie with the Royal House of Raza!

Whoever it was who was terrorizing her knew what that connection was with the Royal Family. Did Fuchsia stand to gain something if this connection were proved? That could only be the answer. But how and what she had no idea. She suddenly realized how late it was. It had been late when she met Lucien in the garden. She looked at her watch, the hands pointed to one in the morning! The realization came to her of how silent the castle was, no distant murmur of servants voices - for naturally they were all in bed. Then the lights went out. Fuchsia stood, as if made of stone like the little mermaid in the garden, a shaft of moonlight shone on the terrible eyes of Anna Theresa, illuminating them until they were two terrifying pinpoints of black light - then they were veiled by a dark shadow passing over the portrait. Then a dark something moved within inches of where the paralyzed girl stood, something that emanated hatred and hung heavy on the air of the room like a sickening odor. Then the hatred was rent by an unearthly screech, followed by threatening growls and with a terrible hiss something launched itself through the air at the dark something, tearing at the unseen visage. To Fuchsia came the sound of muffled oaths in a recognizably human voice and the angry yowls of 'Tiger' thought Fuchsia in almost hysterical relief. A furry body flung itself against her legs, with a rough purr deep in his throat. Her unseen enemy had once more been thwarted, thanks to an adoring cat that had the thankful habit of following her about.

The lights went on again in the gallery; she was alone with Tiger who stared up at his beloved, eyes like twin green lamps. She picked him up and a rough tongue licked her nose perhaps for once imagining himself to be canine rather than feline!

It was midday when Fuchsia stirred, a loud knocking on the door, she got out of bed, slightly dazed, the door had, of course, been locked, after the sinister events of last night. When she opened the door, it was to find Greta, looking anxious.

"What is it?" Fuchsia asked.

"Well nothing, exactly, Madam," answered the maid, but went on, "only when I came earlier, I was worried because you did not answer!"

"Of course, that was thoughtless of me," apologized Fuchsia, "I'm afraid I simply overslept."

"Will you still require breakfast," enquired Greta with a gleam of amusement in the depths of her eyes.

"Er - no, better make it lunch," answered the girl with a smile.

The maid turned to go and then paused...

"Oh - there was one thing Madam..."

"Yes."

"Well one of the servants saw lights going on and off in the picture gallery, very late last night, we thought it might be a burglar, which was one reason why we were worried when you did not answer. There have been other things too..."

"As a matter of fact," Fuchsia said, "I was in the picture gallery last night, so that would account for the lights going on and off." She did not add that there had been a near further attempt on her life. "But what do you mean by other things?" The maid looked away, confused, "Go on, don't be afraid," encouraged the girl.

"Well it's not so much that I'm afraid Madam but that you might think me rather silly."

"Never mind, carry on," answered Fuchsia, trying to conceal her impatience.

"The servants including myself have seen a shadowy figure at night in the grounds and in the more deserted corridors and strange noises coming from rooms where they used..."

"Who are 'they' Greta?" Fuchsia almost snapped at her, "and used to what?" Greta went a shade paler.

"Well... er..."

"Come along?" said Fuchsia, completely losing patience. The maid gave in with a sigh.

"Well if I really must tell you Madam, 'they' are Queen Caroline Rose and the artist who came to paint her portrait, with whom she fell in love, Jean Pierre, and I was speaking of the various places where they were supposed to have met."

"I see, but what has this to do with burglars and strange noises?" inwardly guessing the answer. Greta stared at the ground, almost embarrassed.

"It is said that the ghosts of the Queen and her lover return to the scenes of their happiness, trying to recapture their love in eternity."

"And has anyone seen these ghosts?" questioned Fuchsia eagerly. The maid looked directly into her eyes then.

"Although such people as servants have sworn they have heard things, the legend says that only persons of royal blood, who are related to the Queen, have the power to see her." A kind of shock went through the English girl at that particular piece of information.

"Has the King seen her?" asked Fuchsia breathlessly.

"Not the King," Greta paused, "but my mother, who was house-keeper in the palace when the King was a child, once told me that his mother, the late Queen Zenobia, saw her several times, not only here, but at that hotel which was once Caroline Rose's villa, and always dressed as she is in the portrait downstairs. She saw her usually when there was some crisis or danger in her life, such as the time when she first came to the throne and a Communist tried to shoot her, she told her husband a long time afterwards that an unknown hand had pushed her to the ground, yet there was no-one by her time at the time, and the bullet just whizzed harmlessly over her head, and the man was, amazingly, the one who tried to kill her that is, lying dead, not from the bullets of the bodyguards as you might expect but he had had a massive heart attack probably immediately after firing the bullet. Queen Zenobia also said later that at the second she was pushed down, she saw fleetingly the sparkle of stars and the sheen of silk, looking very like a certain gown!"

Fuchsia was lost in thought for a moment, and then straightened herself. "Thank you for telling me all this Greta, that will be all for now." The maid gave a slight curtsey and left the room.

The girl walked across to the window, and gazed at the lake. So the only people who were able to see the ghost of Caroline Rose were those who had royal blood in their veins, who were of the House of Raza! This bore out the suspicion even more that Fuchsia herself had a connection by blood with the dead Queen, for had she not seen her at least once... or perhaps twice... for she was now beginning to believe that the same hand that had once saved Zenobia from assassination had also saved Fuchsia from being stabbed to death! And then another revelation flashed across her mind. The veiled figure who had tried to kill her, whom she now suspected was feminine, judging by the muffled shriek, that very shriek proved that the unknown killer had seen Fuchsia's rescuer, had recognized that rescuer, and incredible though it seemed, if that rescuer had indeed been the kindly spirit of Caroline Rose, then the person who had tried to kill Fuchsia on that and other occasions must also be of royal blood!

The girl's heart leapt with sudden relief, then perhaps after all it was not Alex who was trying to kill her... unless... and her heart thudded in heartbreaking panic once more, unless, as was likely, as Lucien had suggested, there was more than one person involved, perhaps even three, and one of those persons might be the unknown woman... an evil, ruthless woman in the life of a murderous King?

Chapter 9

There was another knock at the door. "Come in," Fuchsia called. Greta re-entered the room, carrying an envelope in her hand. She walked over to Fuchsia who stared at the envelope in curiosity.

"A letter has come for you Madam, delivered by hand to the Palace, with the instruction that no-one but myself should give you the letter."

"Who brought it?" the girl questioned. The maid shrugged in that typically foreign way.

"A young boy... just an ordinary looking teenage boy, he had been told that he would be given a generous tip he delivered straight away. So the gatekeeper tipped him."

"Do you know who sent the letter?" Fuchsia asked.

"No Madam, I'm sorry, I do not know who sent it... but here it is Madam." Fuchsia took the letter from the maid and dismissed her, forcing herself not to slit the envelope until Greta had closed the door behind her. Then she ripped it open in excitement. It was, as she had half expected, a message from Lucien. He had not wasted any time.

'Dear Fuchsia', it read, 'I expect you realize by now that was on to some vital information last night, when you mentioned the name of your great grandmother. I felt it was better to communicate what I have discovered by writing to you, as it may be wise I feel not to be seen together - and in fact DESTROY THIS NOTE AFTER READING IT - this is very important. Now for my findings. When you mentioned the name Gentian, something I had long ago forgotten came back to me. In Switzerland, many years ago, there was a painter, she became famous for painting alpine flowers, including her namesake. Although she lived in Switzerland, she was English born, her name was Gentian Rawlings. I visited the library here in Raza, and it appears she was born about 1860, married in her late thirties, and produced possibly one child around the age of forty. She visited Russia in 1917 and was never heard of again!

With mounting excitement Fuchsia read the note again and again, until she knew it by heart. Then very deliberately she tore it into tiny pieces, walked with them to the nearby bathroom and flushed them down the toilet, watching them until they were swirled out of sight.

Back in her room, she went through the facts in her mind. This woman Gentian, who was her great grandmother disappeared in Russia in 1917 - the year of the Russian Revolution - was there some connection? Did she just drop from sight as the Czar and his family had done together with many other ordinary people?

Fuchsia's glance fell on some of her painting equipment. From this Gentian then came Fuchsia's ability to draw and paint. Apparently the name of the man she had married was unknown. The child she had borne was Fuchsia's grandmother - and the name of the man she had married was also unknown. So much mystery to unravel. Fuchsia decided to have a break from it all, she put on an old overall and went back to work on her portrait of Alex, in an adjoining room where her easel had been set up. Most of the equipment she was using had been purchased locally and brought to the castle, for naturally she had not brought any equipment on holiday with her apart from a sketch pad and pencil which she always carried with her. On holiday - that holiday seemed a million years ago. So much had happened since she had boarded that coach in London.

When was Alex? Had he really gone to Paris? Fuchsia sometimes had the strangest feeling that he was far closer than Paris, but that was probably her imagination. No doubt he often travelled on matters of state, she would have to get used to that - if she lived long enough - and she shivered. Something sharp sank into her ankle. She jumped, dropping her paintbrush, her heart lurched sickeningly. Then the girl looked down and sighed with relief. It was Tiger hooking his claws 'affectionately' into the side of her slipper.

Fuchsia squatted on all fours and stroked him, only then did she notice something hanging from the cat's mouth.

"What have you got there Tiger," she said, amused. The cat gave a playful growl in reply as his mistress gave a gentle tug at what appeared to be a piece of string in Tiger's mouth. The cat bit her fingers gently and dropped the 'string'. Fuchsia picked it up.

The 'string' was in fact a string of tiny ivory beads, which no doubt the cat had found somewhere and had played with them.

Fuchsia remembered at other times seeing Tiger play with items of jewelry, particularly necklaces, for which he possessed a particular liking, pawing them and biting them. On several occasions she had caught him with her own pearls which had belonged to her grandmother, and had quickly hoisted them to safety, for who could deny even pearls to an animal that had saved her life? He often jumped onto her dressing table, playing with various odds and ends of jewelry. She took another look at the ivory beads; her trained eye noted their superb quality, and their probably fairly considerable value, for they were certainly very old. She doubted that they belonged to any of the maids, for apart from Greta, they were all peasant women and Greta did not wear jewelry. No member of the Royal Family was in the palace apart from herself, there were no guests. So whose were they? Had the cat found them in one of the old rooms perhaps? No - they had the feeling of a living person. She dismissed the beads for the time being and placed them at the back of a drawer beneath some handkerchiefs. Her thoughts once more returned to the mystery she seemed to be the centre of. Was it Alex who wanted her out of the way? It was possible. He had a motive. Yet something deep inside her convinced her of his innocence, and that something was her discovery of the type of woman his mother had been. Zenobia and Caroline Rose, though perhaps only distantly related, had the same kind of radiance that shines long after they are gone from this world. What was this radiance? It was not the radiance of physical beauty though they had that too. It was a kind of inner radiance, because they were good women in the sense that they loved deeply and saw the beauty that was truth smiling serenely amidst life's cruelties, to ultimately banish those tears with the musical laugh of love.

Such a woman could not have produced a murderer. Fuchsia had returned to her bedroom to put away the mysterious beads, and at the end of her contemplation, her eyes caught sight of a photograph album which Alex had pointed out. She had briefly looked at some photographs of Alex as a child with his parents, one with his long dead Alsatian, Hercules, and many other typical family photographs that families possess, Royal or ordinary alike. There was even a rather stiff Victorian photograph of Caroline Rose at the age of around twelve with her father. Fuchsia looked at it with interest. Even in that ancient faded photograph, that radiant beauty already peeped through. She turned the pages, various names took on faces, Anna Maria's half-sister, Carlotta Elisabeth, and the latter's daughter Elsa Theresa who became the second wife of Anna Maria's son, Jan VI. Next was a portrait of Princess Irene, aged twenty, their daughter, half-sister of Zenobia and aunt to Alex. Fuchsia studied it and she was suddenly very still. This was the first time she had seen Princess Irene closely, for when she passed in the carriage, she had only gained a fleeting impression of her features, and then of course she was elderly. But here in the blossoming of early youth was a good-looking dark haired girl - with - Fuchsia's heart missed a beat - with the same repellant cold eyes of her forbear - Anna Theresa!

A line from the book in the library flashed back into Fuchsia's mind. 'The mother of Anna Theresa, Giulia Caravari was descended from the Medici's and the Borgia's.' So also did this woman Irene have the blood of the Borgia's in her veins! Had not many of the Borgia's been mad!

MAD... the word suddenly screamed around the room. Fuchsia went very cold. Almost mechanically she picked up a pencil and notepad and wrote the words as far as she remembered them from the piece of paper which must have been torn from a diary. 'I sense her hatred... and I am afraid... I believe my father was right about her... why did I not listen to him... to his warnings that she...' Fuchsia looked at the photograph of Princess Irene and completed the sentence in the diary by adding 'that she was MAD' That was it.

The girl knew as surely as if someone had whispered it in her ear. Anna Theresa had been insane - and Fuchsia realized now - completely evil. But she had not been insane in a maniacal sense. Her madness had channeled itself into a brilliantly clever brain to organize murderous intrigue in an insatiable desire for power. Her blood had been well schooled by a certain Cesare Borgia.

What was more - the madness that had been transmitted across four hundred years to Anna Theresa now stared at her from the eyes of Princess Irene!

Fuchsia looked away from the photograph of Princess Irene and her eyes suddenly rested once more on the photograph of Caroline Rose and her father, Frederick III, and a little more of the puzzle fell into place. The page from the diary had been written by Caroline Rose. She had been warned by her father, probably as he lay dying, that her aunt was insane. If anyone knew the woman was insane, it would be her half-brother, the King. No wonder he had excluded her from the succession should his daughter die without issue. The throne was to pass, and did pass to his niece, Anna Maria.

But then another perplexing question flashed into Fuchsia's mind to add to the tangle of riddles. Had not King Frederick considered that even if he excluded the mother, her daughter might be tainted with the same madness? So why leave the throne to a niece who was equally likely to become insane. It had certainly passed through his younger niece down to Princess Irene. Had it by-passed Anna Maria by sheer luck? On a sudden impulse Fuchsia flew along to the library, and took out the book from where she had pushed it. She opened it at the royal family tree. The father of Anna Maria had been an Italian Marquis who died when his daughter was hardly born. His widow married again very soon afterwards one of their many cousins, who became the father of Irene's grandmother, Carlotta Elisabeth. Two slightly odd facts stood out from the family tree and the detailed information within the pages. Anna Theresa had been married ten years before the birth of Anna Maria, and her brother had removed the little girl from her mother's household when she was only a year old, the year of Caroline Rose's birth. Why? Did he fear she would harm the child, knowing of the mother's madness - OR - and the answer seemed to be whispered to her again – it was possible the child was not hers at all! Then if Anna Maria was not the daughter of Anna Theresa - whose daughter was she? Suddenly remembering the torn page from the diary she looked at the place in the book where she had hidden it. It was still there!

She took it out and carefully put it in her pocket. Fuchsia then studied the book in more detail, particularly on the section about Frederick III. He had married his English wife in 1839 - when he was nearing the age of thirty - a rather late age for marrying in those days and for someone in his position. Fuchsia read on. In 1838-1839 he had been involved in a scandal - hence the possible reason for his sudden marriage. The scandal was that he had become violently infatuated (a man who up to that time by all accounts had been something of a prude) with a beautiful opera singer - a woman who was half gypsy. He even wanted to marry her, but his trusted advisers soon put a stop to that by pointing out where his duty lay. The gypsy singer who really cared nothing for the King was paid off and sent away, but before she left she presented the King with a daughter - and there the narrative ended. Over the page an old painting showed the beautiful gypsy in an operatic role - the face was that of Anna Maria! Another piece of the puzzle fell into place in Fuchsia's mind. So Anna Maria was the daughter of King Frederick - Caroline Rose's own half sister! No wonder the King had wanted her to succeed him should anything happen to his legitimate daughter. He had obviously got around the legitimacy issue by forcing Anna Theresa to accept the child as her own daughter. How she must have hated him!

Chapter 10

By sheer accident Fuchsia's eyes swept once more over the photograph of Princess Irene and another piece of the puzzle clicked into place. She knew the identity of the person who had tried to kill her in the Portrait Gallery! She took the beads that the cat had found and compared them with the ones around the neck of Princess Irene in the photograph. They were remarkably alike! Was Princess Irene the unknown would-be assassin?

At that moment Greta walked into the room - and stopped when she saw Fuchsia.

"Oh excuse me Madam," she apologized, "I did not know you were here."

"That's quite alright Greta," Fuchsia smiled.

"Tell me Greta," she said carefully, "have you ever seen much of Princess Irene?" The maid looked up - surprised at the question.

"Well Madam, I have seen her on the occasions she has visited the castle, but... well... that is not often... she and the King do not get on well together."

"Oh – I did not know that," answered Fuchsia. She held up the beads. "Do you happen to know if Princess Irene has ever worn these beads?" The maid looked.

"But Madam - those beads surely belong to Baroness Elsa?"

Elsa - Fuchsia was as still as the statue of the little mermaid in the garden. Princess Irene and Elsa... both had motive and opportunity. On the part of Elsa it was jealous disappointment. One thing however did not quite fit. Granted that Princess Irene and Elsa could have joined forces for mutual satisfaction - but why should Elsa be wearing Princess Irene's beads? Irene did not strike Fuchsia as a woman who would be generous, and she could not imagine Elsa appreciating any act of generosity.

So lost in thought was she that she had forgotten that Greta was still in the room. Fuchsia looked round at the maid.

"Tell me Greta - why do you think that Baroness Elsa would be wearing a necklace which…" pointing to the photograph, "obviously belongs to Princess Irene?" Greta walked across and glanced at the picture. She looked at Fuchsia.

"Then you obviously do not know Madam - the King only knew six months ago."

"Know what Greta?" enquired Fuchsia with a dawning suspicion at the back of her mind. Greta answered.

"Although it is not known outside palace circles, and as I said the true facts were not even known by the King until six months ago… thirty and more years ago, Princess Irene, who was not so young herself by then, fell in love with an Austrian baron. He however was married, and he was a Catholic, so he could not divorce his wife. Also his wife was an invalid, there were no children of the marriage. He and the Princess had an affair, and a child resulted. The Queen Zenobia had the child removed, she said there was some slight instability in Irene. The baron's wife got to know about the child and she offered to forgive her husband and bring the child up as her own. The Queen consented - and the baron adopted his own daughter - that daughter was Elsa."

At last some of the final pieces were falling into place. However Fuchsia held her astonishment in check.

"Why did Al… I mean the King only discover these facts six months ago Greta?"

"Because Princess Irene only chose to disclose her secret after certain pressure had been put on her by the King. It seems that the King had come across some papers and documents in his mother's handwriting by accident. At the time there was talk of his engagement to Baroness Elsa. He had met her at some embassy function in Vienna, and of course at the time he had no reason to believe that there was any connection between Elsa and his aunt. Though when he invited Elsa to stay at the palace, his aunt did admit to knowing her parents in the past. Then one morning the King came to her apartments in a terrible rage, I believe she was very frightened when he presented her with the documents. So she confessed to her secret. It was then that privately the King broke off his engagement."

"And did Elsa know that she was Irene's daughter?"

"Not apparently until the King informed her of the contents of the papers. But there was certainly a terrible scene between him and Elsa. Their voices rang around the palace. In the end she ran out to her car in hysterics." Fuchsia then dismissed the maid and began to consider the latest startling facts. She at once guessed that it was on the cards that Elsa had known of the relationship between herself and the King's aunt. She and the old lady must have engineered the whole thing right down to the original meeting between herself and Alex. What a calamity had they married. The seeds of madness would have joined with the main bloodlines! No wonder he had been angry. Had he known about the madness? What had been in the papers that Zenobia had had the foresight to leave behind? She too must have known about the taint of madness. Zenobia had had the child adopted, so there was absolutely no chance of it making any claims to the throne.

A lot of the facts now seemed to fall into place. The family had for over a hundred and fifty years harbored an evil spirit among its noble branches. The evil spirit that had entered the day Giulia Caravari became the stepmother of Frederick III. Hatred, born of inherent madness was passed from mother to child, from one generation to another. She saw now that it must have been Elsa Theresa, the mother of Princess Irene who had engineered the attempt on the life of Zenobia, using as a screen, the time when communism had reared its ugly head in a royalist state.

Elsa Theresa had lived until the late nineteen twenties, plenty of time to have engineered such an attempt on her stepdaughter's life. Had it succeeded, no-one would have opposed the natural accession of Irene, for Zenobia was then childless. Only one person could have opposed that right and that was the vanished daughter of Caroline Rose, although that daughter would by then have been a woman in her sixties, if she was alive. She might also have had children.

Had Elsa Theresa and Irene known of the whereabouts of that daughter? These were questions that had yet to be answered. But the answers to such questions were not as important as safeguarding Fuchsia's life. A revelation suddenly presented itself in her mind, not in a world shattering way, just calmly and quietly as it had been waiting for this moment all her life. It was so simple Fuchsia almost laughed. She knew it for the truth, almost as if it had been whispered in her ear. It was the key to the whole mystery, the key to the attempts on her life. It was that Gentian Rawlings - an artist - was the vanished daughter of Caroline Rose, Queen of Karolia, and the artist - Jean Pierre. She Fuchsia was the great great granddaughter of Caroline Rose and Jean Pierre - she Fuchsia - also an artist.

Later that evening , Greta brought Fuchsia a local herbal drink which the girl had come to like very much. She usually had it last thing at night. There was a soothing quality to it that swept her along on the tide of sleep.

Tonight however, after she had finished drinking and prepared for bed, she felt unusually drowsy, and her eyelids felt like lead, yet they did not close as they might have done with such a feeling of drowsiness. Tiger lay under the bed, purring rhythmically.

The purring seemed to grow louder and her eyelids began to grow heavier. She switched off the light, opened the doors onto the balcony, and the cool night air rushed into the room. Across the lake golden lights winked and shone from isolated hamlets in the mountains, and the lake shimmered in a silvery green luminosity.

Hypnotized by the view before her and the gentle fresh breeze against her skin, Fuchsia stood in a state where she was not quite sure if she was dreaming or awake, where enchantment blurred reason at the edges of consciousness, seeming to mingle with the silver waters of the lake. Did strong arms steal around her waist? Did hard lips descend on her own to which she responded with passion long denied. Did a dangerous flame burn in the depths of a man's dark eyes with an exciting promise which made her blood throb with a heady delight, making her senses swim in an insane exhilaration? Then she was sinking sinking into the lake of a dreamless sleep... the last thing she remembered was of a soft coverlet being placed over her... someone closing the windows against the freshening breeze and then... oblivion.

She rose the next morning with sunshine pouring into the room. She felt sluggish and almost depressed - yet - strangely excited. Had her usual herbal drink been drugged? Fuchsia thought it was likely. But for what reason? She flushed as she remembered the sensations of the previous night. Had that all been a dream, a figment of imagination conjured up by a drugged sleep. Her heart told her that it was real... a man had held her in his arms... that man could only be the one her heart and senses responded to. Even in a state of near sleep she knew who it was. It was the man she loved... the man she had married only a short time before... Alex... whispered her heart.

It must have been Alex or at least by his order that the drink had been treated. Why? There could only be one answer. For some reason he did not want it to be known that he was in the vicinity. Did he not even want Fuchsia to be sure it was he. To all intents and purposes he was in Paris. Fuchsia remembered the times in the past days when she had sensed him to be near. Now she knew she had been right, did he know of her danger? Intuition told her that he did and that it was not him she had to fear. Suddenly the knowledge that Alex knew of her danger seemed to lift a great weight from her heart. The depression lifted and she saw the friendly sparrows chirping as they hopped along the edge of the balcony. Crumbs of biscuits or chocolate were now a daily ritual and their bright eyes seemed to be seeking her intently through the glass.

"Patience - little friends," Fuchsia called, laughingly as she slid from the warmth of the bed. She opened the window and put the remains of some cake she had saved for them on the balcony rail, and watched in amusement as they snapped them up greedily in their sharp little beaks.

When she had finished watching the sparrows she went along to the bathroom, quickly washed and came back to the bedroom and dressed as speedily. She felt an uplift of pure happiness in spite of the past days of mystery and fear.

She now at least believed she knew why the attempts were being made on her life. If, as she now felt fairly certain, she - Fuchsia, was the great great granddaughter of Caroline Rose, then obviously she was the one who was entitled to that lady's fortune - therefore she must be eliminated. Yet even with Fuchsia out of the way - there was still Alex. Even a slightly insane person like Princess Irene would no doubt see that it was not a terribly good idea to murder the King as well as Fuchsia. So what was the alternative? The alternative was naturally that Elsa would marry Alex, for they obviously presumed that he knew nothing of their murderous intentions, at least up to the time he had discovered the documents left by Zenobia. Then everything had changed.

Even had Alex still been ignorant of their plans, how would they force him to marry Elsa? Fuchsia had no doubt that Irene would find a way. She was not her ancestor Anna Theresa all over again for nothing. But at least Fuchsia now felt sure that Alex knew, had known all along their evil plotting. She knew that she was not - had never been – quite along during the past days.

It was like being in a maze where one could not find the entrance or exit - then afterwards - from the air - one could see every avenue and twist and turn for what it really was – one single thread forced into a tangle to be pulled straight again.

So lost was she in her thoughts and revelations that she not look where she was going and her leg bumped against the old chest at the foot of the bed, the chest that contained the dress of Caroline Rose. There was a sharp click, Fuchsia gasped in amazement, a kind of secret drawer slid slowly open by itself in the seemingly solid base of the chest. The girl's clumsiness had accidentally pressed the mechanism which operated the drawer. There was something dark in the surrounding darkness inside the drawer.

Fuchsia lowered herself slowly to her knees and cautiously felt inside the drawer. Her hand encountered what appeared to be a small pile of books. She pulled them out. They were leather bound diaries. Fuchsia placed them on the bed with a strange trembling excitement. She opened the first diary - inside as she had half expected, there was some handwriting – the same handwriting that had been on the scrap of paper in the library, and her was the proof. In exactly the same handwriting and on exactly the same kind of paper she read: 'Caroline Rose - Diary for the year 1854'. Fuchsia suddenly noticed what she had almost stupidly missed before. The language which was used by Caroline Rose in her diaries including the few words on the scrap of paper in the library - was English. It had just not occurred to Fuchsia before that the torn page was in English and not Karolian.

Perhaps it was not so unusual that Caroline Rose had written it in English rather than Karolian, because she had most probably been bilingual, having an English mother. From what she had heard Fuchsia knew that the dead Queen had been fluent in French, German, Italian and Spanish also.

English, however, would not have been as widely spoken as for instance German or French in an out of the way place like Karolia in the middle years of the last century, so it was possible that she had used English, because anyone else curious or with motive to read her diaries would be less likely to be able to understand English than any of the other mentioned languages.

The diary for 1854 was not particularly interesting. It had been written when Caroline Rose's father was still alive. Her handwriting, though recognizable as hers, still had a childish look and the everyday events which she described, such as the lessons she had with her French governess etc, were written in an immature style, for at time she was still only fourteen years old.

Yet though still so young, the radiant warmth of her personality shone through the dust of time to touch the heart of her great great granddaughter. Fuchsia put the 1854 diary to one side and searched for the one for 1855. 1855 was the year Caroline Rose succeeded to the throne. But there was no missing page. They were all intact. Which was the most likely diary to have a page missing? The year 1858 came unbidden to the girl's mind. That was the year Caroline Rose met Jean Pierre. She opened the 1858 diary.

Sure enough the page for the first of September had been ripped out, immediately below the date!

Who had torn out the sheet of paper? Whoever it was knew these diaries were here in the secret drawer. Was it Princess Irene or her daughter? The answers to many questions were probably in the pages of these diaries. Fuchsia made a sudden decision. She took all the diaries from off the bed and going over to the place where her suitcase was stored, she opened the case, and placed the diaries in two neat rows at the bottom and covered them over with some spare items of clothing and large beach towel. She closed the lid, fetched the keys from her handbag and locked the case securely, replacing in the storage area. If the unknown person came back for the diaries they would have an unpleasant surprise. Another thought struck Fuchsia: they would also guess that she had discovered theme!

Fuchsia could not help wondering why Zenobia, as she had known of the streak of insanity in her half-sister, why she had not had her sister put away perhaps in some kind of clinic where, even if they were unable to help her, she would have ceased to be a danger to anyone. Surely she should have been placed somewhere before she had had time to produce child who could transmit the insanity to another generation. Of course on the other hand, insane people were clever enough to conceal their insanity from the rest of the world. It would have had to be proved that she was mad, and no doubt Irene was too cunning to have placed herself in the position where doctors would have signed away her freedom. No - Zenobia eventually knew but could never prove that there was a nest of vipers within the nest itself, she could only try and prevent, take precautions and give warning to her son.

Where would it all end? Which party would triumph? A sudden breath of wind stirred the curtains, and a soft sound seemed to vibrate through the room... almost like someone sighing. Fuchsia turned to the window almost as if some force beyond herself was urging her to look. Paralyzed with shock, against the balcony a now familiar figure was outlined, the sunlight seeming to catch the glints in the lustrous chestnut hair. On her hand sat a living dove, pink-white in the sunshine. The figure raised her hand to her face and lightly kissed the soft feathers of the dove and replaced it on the edge of the balcony where it pecked at some crumbs as the figure faded. Totally unafraid, Fuchsia knew that Caroline Rose had shown her the dove as a message of peace - and hope.

Fuchsia felt absolutely no fear. Yet she knew that the times she had seen Caroline Rose were by no means a product of the imagination. The materialization half way through the twentieth century of a long dead woman was real enough to have held a living dove, real enough to have deflected a knife to save the life of a descendant born nearly a century after her own death. Real enough perhaps to have once also saved the life of Zenobia.

Something in Caroline Rose could not rest - not until the knowledge that once only she possessed was made known - and the cause of that knowledge stamped out forever. So strong was the love of this woman for her daughter and the heirs of that daughter's own body - that something of her lived on - something of her that no-one in this world could explain - but that something would go on protecting - maybe just for now - maybe forever - but the spirit of Caroline Rose would never die and be lost in the emptiness of the universe.

Fuchsia woke from her thoughts as if from a dream and saw that the dove had gone. It too had shown no fear, but it was aware of a loving presence that held it, felt the loving lips of that presence for the persecuted furred and feathered creatures of this world. The dove had shown perfect trust.

In a room not far from where Fuchsia was, two of her enemies faced each other. The one was a handsome elderly lady - kindly an onlooker might think until he came close - when he would recoil in horror - at the total darkness with a gleam of fanatical light in her dark eyes. The eyes would remind him of the portrait in another part of the castle.

The other person in the room would only be seen as a grey shape by the onlooker. The curtains were drawn, as the old lady could not stand the strong light of day, and the grey shape stood in the darkest part of the room, speaking in muffled tones. Even the sex of the other person would be difficult to say on the part of an onlooker. But the old lady knew this person very well - very well indeed!

The old woman spoke: "So she has found the diaries! We need not worry about that. I tore out the valuable piece of evidence - or rather she did." She nodded contemptuously towards a third person sitting some distance away. It was a young woman with a look of the old lady about her. The grey shape said: "where's the paper," directing their voice at the girl. Trickles of sweat suddenly ran down the body of the girl - she was mortally afraid of the grey shape - for she suddenly remembered - she no longer had the paper - could not even remember what she had done with it!

"I don't know where it is," the girl replied in a hoarse whisper. A horrific sound like the snarl of a wild animal came from the grey shape. As silent and as slowly as a ghost the shape took one step at a time towards the girl.

"What are you going to do?" shouted the old lady. Hideous shrieks issued from the lips of the girl as she tore at the scarf which slowly tightened around her throat. The shrieks petered out into a choking gurgle and her hands flopped to her sides as her lifeless body slipped to the floor.

"No…" shrieked the old lady as the grey shape turned towards her…

Fuchsia, to take her mind temporarily from her problems had begun some painting. She was completely absorbed in her task and did not notice until the light began to fade that she must have been working steadily for about five hours. The castle was strangely quiet, even for this wing, and she suddenly realized that no-one had called her to lunch or tea. A small flicker of alarm went through her. Where was everybody? Where was Greta? Only Tiger lay on the bed dreaming… Suddenly, close to her room, she caught muffled sounds - voices perhaps and a thumping noise. On an impulse - though for what actual reason she could not analyze - and sensing danger to herself, she at the same time sensed danger to the animal on the bed. She picked up the cat and crept into the corridor. Farther down there were some unused bedrooms into which one day she had idly looked.

In one was a small room which had once been a powder closet. Inside was an old couch, a small table and some chairs. She hurriedly placed Tiger on the old couch, then locked the door of the small room, taking the key, and finally locking the outer bedroom door. She then hid the keys under the floor covering of a clothes closet in the bedroom two doors away.

Whoever her enemy was, they did not like cats, especially after being attacked by Tiger. So she did not want Tiger around for what she felt was to be the final confrontation whether or not she would come out of it herself. She walked in the direction from which the sounds came, back towards the main part of the castle - but still a great distance from the servants.

She came to the apartment which she had been told was Princess Irene's on her extremely rare visits to her nephew. Strange - the door was ajar. They were usually kept locked except when the maids entered to dust. Fuchsia pushed open the door further, the room was in total darkness, particularly with the curtains drawn right across the window.

For the second time that day Fuchsia stumbled into something, it was soft and gave at the touch of her foot. A sudden sick feeling welled up inside her. She backed away to the door and fumbled for the light switch. It flicked on and the girl's mouth opened in a silent scream. On the floor the auburn hair partly hiding her distorted features, lay the body of the girl Fuchsia had known as Elsa, Baroness von Kelberg, illegitimate daughter of Princess Irene. There was never any doubt in the mind of Fuchsia that she was dead. In the armchair, slumped forward, was the mother of the dead girl, Princess Irene no less, also quite dead. Nearby lay a scarf - the two women had been strangled. A terrible fear shot through the girl in the doorway, the two people she had assumed to be her arch enemies were dead, therefore someone who was a far greater enemy had put an end to them. The hand of someone gave her a shove in the small of her back so that she fell forward into the room.

She picked herself up slowly turned around hardly daring to look, strangely calm now that she was at last to be face to face with her unknown enemy. But when her eyes alighted on the familiar features, her brain reeled in shock. Never in all her imaginings had she guessed that it could be... 'Lucien'!

"Yes - dear Fuchsia – Lucien!" he pushed her down into a chair. Then he took from his pocket two scraps of paper and fitted them together. It was the complete page from the old diary. The part that Fuchsia had discovered and the part that had been ripped from the bottom thus completing the sentence – 'that she... is mad'! The man held them up in front of Fuchsia so that she could read it.

"Yes - Queen Fuchsia - dear Caroline Rose was right - my great great grandmother was mad – mad with power – power that will be rightfully mine." The girl's brain once more reeled with shock.

"Your..." she could not finish the sentence.

"How astonished you must be," continued the man in chilling sarcasm. That is where good old Zenobia made her big mistake. She thought her half sister had one stupid daughter - that one down there," he laughed, kicking at the body of Elsa. "What she did not know was that Irene had TWINS - a boy and a girl, yes, that..." once more kicking at the body of his sister, "is my twin. Irene was far more clever than she was given credit for, she let Zenobia take away the girl, but the boy - myself was smuggled out to England - adopted by a couple who taught me the full knowledge of who I was. When I grew up my mother and I planned a nice little take-over of the country, planned a nice little departure from this world of dear cousin Alex. Unfortunately we overlooked the fact that Zenobia had left certain papers so that her arrogant son stumbled onto our secret. Then we found the diaries and you had to come on the scene. We planned to eliminate you as well as the King.

What we did not bargain for was that the philandering King would fall for you and marry you! It may interest you to know that your great grandmother Gentian married a Russian, and she was brought up on the estate of her great grandfather, the Duke of Berrington. Your grandmother married a son of the later Duke of Berrington, but he left her, which facts made our job tougher because my dear your ancestors were all legitimate issue!

Fuchsia, in a complete state of shock suddenly began to function again. "So it was you with the knife in the gallery, and your sister playing the harpsichord - and of course you engineered the mermaid incident."

"Of course - what else? Except that the idiot of my sister ruined the first attempt by saying she had seen a ghost of that old Queen. So it is now up to me to successfully complete our mission. The girl could now see the same insane fanaticism in his eyes, though unlike his mother and sister, his eyes were grey. But the light of madness in his eyes was magnified a thousand times - was in fact completely evil to murder his mother and sister even though they were all chips off the old block in the person of Anna Theresa! He picked up the scarf from the floor and started towards Fuchsia. She stood rigid with terror - then suddenly the light went out. She felt the swish of a silken skirt against her ankles and a pair of loving arms pulling her down down into comforting darkness and oblivion... a shot rang out... and oblivion...

When Fuchsia awoke, the first thing she saw was the body of Lucien on the floor, a red stain spreading across his chest, and like his relatives, quite dead. The room seemed to be full of police. She looked up into the beloved features of Alex who held her in his arms. "Why did you go away, when I was in such danger?"

"But I didn't my darling, I was near you all the time, forgive me, but we had to use you as bait. We discovered a long time ago the plots of these three. Oh yes (seeing her questioning look) we knew about Lucien. Elsa was very talkative when she had had too much to drink. He was the one unfortunate fact my mother overlooked, everything else, your personal history we found through detective work - you - my dearest are a very rich woman - and the skeleton in the cupboard of the House of Raza has gone forever..." and any other information was halted by more pleasant pursuits as his mouth came closer, and Fuchsia smiled a little at the memory of a silken skirt and loving arms.

One year later, Princess Caroline Rose Zenobia, heiress to the throne of Karolia, had just returned from her Christening and now lay sleeping in a cradle of silk and lace, facing the lake in the room that had been that of Caroline Rose. She suddenly opened her very blue eyes and chestnut curls bobbed around the tiny face as she laughed up at someone. On the floor beside the cradle, the green eyes of Tiger the cat, the child's constant companion and protector, gleamed like lamps in a welcome for that someone. At that moment, Fuchsia, newly made Queen and co-sovereign with her husband Alex slipped into the room, in time to see the grown replica of the child in the cradle, in a dress of diamond stars, bend softly and kiss the cheek of her great great great granddaughter. She stroked the soft fur of the cat. Then, blowing a kiss to Fuchsia, and with a peaceful sigh Caroline Rose drifted into a sunbeam which slanted like a golden arm of love across the cradle to eternity.

The End